Excerpt from Christmas Wishes:

She glanced over at the grave where Albert stood, as she tried to hold back her tears. "Was she your wife?"

He sighed. The cloud of his breath swirled in the cold winter air like a scrolling measure of pain.

"She was." He looked at his truck. "I need to go. Someone is waiting for me. Just thought I'd stop by and wish her a Merry Christmas."

A whisper of jealousy crept up her spine, but she ignored it. She had what she wanted; time with Daniel.

"Merry Christmas, Lee. I hope you get everything your heart desires."

CHRISTMAS ROMANCE

DANICA WINTERS

JENNIFER CONNER

SHARON KLEVE

CASEY DAWES

Christmas Wishes
Danica Winters

❖Chapter One❖

A solitary snowflake landed on the pine wreath in Lee Llewellyn's hands. Its lacy white edges curled around the warm boughs like melting fingers, dripping down the pin-point needles and falling unceremoniously to the frozen grass of the cemetery.

The grass crunched under her feet as she made her way to the familiar marble headstone with the bird inscribed in the black-inked stone. Last week's roses lay at the base, their heads drooping in icy lamentation. The aged, brittle roses reminded her of the way she always seemed to feel—frozen in time, waiting for someone to pluck her from her stupor, only to be replaced.

Today the flowers would stay. Lee couldn't bring herself to destroy their despondent beauty. They could stay one more week. Daniel wouldn't mind—or at least, she hoped his spirit wouldn't. In truth, he'd never been one for flowers anyway. If anything, the flowers were more for her, like the wreath in her hands. Curling the velvety red ribbon so it sat perfectly at the center, she laid the circular wreath next to the roses, careful to leave her son's name legible.

She read each word as she had done a thousand times before. Daniel Edward Llewellyn. Born May 10th, 1990. Died December 23, 2010.

The tear trickled down Lee's cheek, unchecked by time or self-control. She couldn't imagine a time when the deep pain of those words would leave her unaffected. Yes, they were only words, little letters etched into stone, but they signified so much pain and so many memories. They meant everything to her, just like Daniel.

A car roared to a stop behind her on the drive. Turning from the grave, she glanced back in time to see a man step out of a mud-covered truck. He caught her gaze and dipped his head. Reaching back into the truck, he pulled out a well-worn black cowboy hat and slipped it over his too-long locks.

Though she didn't recognize the dark-haired man with his stubble-ridden cheeks, flickers of annoyance filled her. He had no right to interfere with her grief and disturb her time with Daniel.

A knot formed in her stomach as the man trudged toward her, as if he was unaware of his intrusion. She tried to get his attention, but the man's hat sat so low on his forehead, she couldn't see his eyes. For a moment she considered calling out and telling him to leave her alone in her sadness, but she stopped. It was Christmas. Since he was here on this day, he must have been enduring the same inescapable agony.

The man moved closer; so close it was almost as if he planned to stand next to her, but he kept walking. A strange disappointment took the place of her annoyance.

He stopped at the third headstone past Daniel's. *Brooke Powers*, Lee recalled. Before she'd picked the plot where her son was laid to rest, she read the headstones of his possible neighbors. If she remembered correctly, Brooke, died at thirty or thereabouts—old enough to keep track of her son's spirit when Lee couldn't be there.

Over the last few years, she'd visited the cemetery each week, but only on holidays did she see flowers on Brooke's headstone. Was this strange cowboy the man who'd brought them? Was he Brooke's husband? Brother? Thin lines collected around his eyes and a few wrinkles decorated his forehead, but he didn't look old enough to be the woman's father.

"Are you going to keep staring at me?" He looked up, catching her off-guard.

"What?" Lee's heart leapt into her throat and a thin sheen of sweat filled her cold hands.

"People only stare at me when I'm in trouble or about to be. Which is it?"

"I don't know what you're talking about. I didn't know I was staring."

"I guess I'm about to be," he answered his own question as his perfect white teeth caught a little ray of winter sun.

"If you are about to be in trouble, than it's trouble of your own doing," she retorted.

"That's funny… That's what Brooke always said." He lifted his chin toward the headstone with the granite angel on top.

"Nice headstone," she said, not quite sure what to say. Grief was a personal thing and, even though he'd

8

brought it up, Lee wasn't sure she wanted to be drawn into a conversation about the loss of loved ones. It would only cause more pain.

"Thanks. Yours too."

She glanced down at the little bird by Danny's name. In truth, her son would have hated it. Her ex-husband picked the bird, and said something to the effect that he and Danny once watched robins together. At the time it seemed wrong to question his memories or his sadness, so the bird had been added to the headstone's order. Danny would have loved something to do with travel. When he wasn't working or going to school, he looked for an adventure. If only he'd been more careful.

"You okay?" the man asked.

Reaching up, Lee touched her fingers to her cheek where she found a tear. "I'm fine."

"I bet." The man walked over and held out his hand. "By the way, I'm Albert Fox. And I'm fine too." He gave a tight laugh.

"I'm Lee… Llewellyn." She slipped her hand in his. His warm fingers circled around her chilled skin.

"Nice to meet you, ma'am."

His hand lingered for a second too long and she pulled away. "You too."

"Heck of a way to spend Christmas Eve, eh?"

She gave a weak smile. "There's nowhere else I'd rather be than with my family."

"Daniel, was your *only* family?" Albert asked, glancing at the headstone.

"He is my son." She thought of her ex-husband and her long-deceased parents. "I'm the only one left."

"I'm sorry to hear that."

There was an awkward silence as he stared at the grave. "I know what it's like to lose someone you love."

He couldn't possibly understand how it felt to have lost her son. He couldn't understand how it felt to give birth to a child. To hold him the second he entered the world and wait for him to take his first breath. To worry from the second he entered the world and then every second after.

She thought back to the day Daniel asked her ex to take the training wheels off his bike when he was only three years old. She had been against it, arguing with her husband that it was too much too soon. *He'll fall. We won't be there to catch him,* she remembered telling him. But he insisted.

They'd spent that night in the ER waiting for Daniel to have his wrist cast.

Then when he'd been eighteen and fresh out of high school Daniel came to them and insisted he wanted to travel the world. He'd asked for the money to fly to England and stay in a hostel. Again, she'd protested. "There's no way you can travel around Europe with no money, no job. You'll fall. We won't be there to catch you."

He'd rolled his eyes and thanked his dad for the cash. That night, she and her ex fought, about the money, and how she resented his intrusion. It was the first fight of many that led to the end of their marriage.

The last time she talked to Daniel, he'd told his father and her about his planned kayaking trip down the

Lochsa River. "It's gonna be a great run," he'd insisted. "Really."

His dad had been all for it, talking about his glory days and how much Daniel would love the thrill of the ride.

"No, Daniel," she'd countered. "It's too dangerous. What happens if you get trapped? You'll fall."

"Let me guess," he'd joked. "No one will be there to catch me."

It turned out that he'd been right. The water had been too much, too fast. There'd been no one there to help him turn in the turbulent rapids of the river.

Now, even though he was gone, she still worried. The feeling never died.

She glanced over at the grave where Albert stood, as she tried to hold back her tears. "Was she your wife?"

He sighed. The cloud of his breath swirled in the cold winter air like a scrolling measure of pain.

"She was." He looked at his truck. "I need to go. Someone is waiting for me. Just thought I'd stop by and wish her a Merry Christmas."

A whisper of jealousy crept up her spine, but she ignored it. She had what she wanted; time with Daniel.

"Merry Christmas, Lee. I hope you get everything your heart desires."

❖Chapter Two❖

How had they gotten into the one conversation that Lee tried to avoid? It was all downhill from there. She kept kicking herself as she made her way to the restaurant. A piece of French Silk pie could cure all that ailed her—or at least she hoped it would.

It had been years since another person—other than her therapist— really talked to her, at least about things that weren't centered on her job, her divorce, or worse—Daniel. Though they talked about Daniel, Albert didn't make a point of talking about her son's death. And there had been something else there. Something made her want to know more about Albert.

She'd been so rude, so stand-offish. It came from years of hiding from her feelings. Years of holding back tears that always threatened to appear out of nowhere and to disappear just as quickly.

She had been self-centered. She'd only focused on her pain. She should have asked him more about his family. More about his Brooke. Maybe he hurt just as bad as she did. Why hadn't she stopped to consider his feelings and what he must have been going through?

Maybe his talking to her was his way of reaching out. Her therapist talked to her about reaching out, at least a thousand times. Each time she nodded and passed the advice off as hogwash, but what if that was what Albert had been doing?

12

She could just kick herself.

The parking lot of the restaurant was full. She parked next to a little Mazda. Its backseat was filled with packages wrapped in red paper with green bows and little sprigs of holly for tags. She glanced into her own empty backseat. She hadn't bought a Christmas present in three years and it would probably be at least a million before she'd buy another one. She had no one left to share a holiday with. No one to share a laugh or a smile.

She was alone.

Alone. Funny how one little word, no, one little *feeling* could encompass it all. Everything she did, everywhere she went. Every word she spoke. It all echoed with that one little word.

For a moment she considered not going into the restaurant. *Party of one.* It would only make her feel the echo more poignantly.

The word hurt. But pie might make it all better— at least for a few minutes. Maybe pie could help her forget the mistakes she'd made with Daniel, her ex, and now Albert.

The door to the restaurant slid shut behind her as she walked to the little wooden podium where the hostess stood.

"Party of one?"

She tried to hold back a cringe, but there was no stopping her response to the woman's unintentional jibe. "No," she said, before she could stop herself. "I'm expecting another."

"Two then. Great," the hostess said absent-mindedly.

Why did Lee say two? She'd have to pretend to wait. How stupid to lie like that. Now it would look as though she'd been stood up.

The hostess grabbed two menus and led her to a booth near the door. Lee slid into the seat nearest the door and took the offered menu while the hostess set the extra menu on the other side of the table.

If she had been ten years younger and a world away, the whole feeling might have been different. She would have reveled in her little façade and hoped Albert would appear and rescue her.

A smile played on her lips as she thought about the dark-haired cowboy with his devilish charm and roguish grace. She could imagine him walking through the doors behind her and saunter up to her table. He would say all the right things. Make her feel as though she was the only woman in the world.

But no. Life was never that easy.

Someone waited for Albert. There was someone who loved him, who probably laughed at his jokes, and who curled up into his arms in the night. He was nothing more than a fantasy. She was too old for those types of dreams. Life had been too hard to allow her to fall for a dream of a future that would never happen.

She couldn't feel sorry for herself. She'd already had a great life. It was easy to forget how wonderful her life had once been, while she sat there alone, and stared at the empty green vinyl bench and the lonesome extra menu.

A waiter with a face so fresh it bordered on pre-pubescent, stopped beside her table. "Hey," the boy said in a monosyllabic grunt. "Can I get you something to drink while you wait?" From the way he stopped short of rolling his eyes, it seemed as though the boy resented being stuck at work on Christmas Eve.

Daniel would have been the same way. He'd always loved Christmas.

"I'll take a cup of coffee and a piece of French Silk pie."

The boy turned and looked over at the roll-top glass refrigerator that held wonderfully cheerful cherry pie, peanut butter pie, lemon meringues, and pies covered with light fluffy cloud-like whipped cream. "Hmmm. I think we're out of French Silk. But we got apple."

Suddenly, it was as though her world collapsed as she stared at the display of joyful pies. The tears flowed unchecked. She tried to stop the flood of misery, but the harder she attempted to stop, the harder she cried. A heaving sob spilled from her as she looked up at the boy who reminded her of Daniel.

The boy's eyes were wide with fear and confusion. "I'm… I'm sorry, ma'am,,." he said in an attempt to comfort her, but it was no use. She was past the point of comfort. "I'll check. Maybe we have a slice in the back."

Before she could stop him to apologize, the boy retreated from the battle zone of her emotions. She couldn't do anything right—not order a slice of pie, not stay married, or save Daniel.

Big fat failure. That's what she was.

Pie couldn't fix that.

Before the waiter could come back and pretend that he hadn't just witnessed her meltdown, Lee escaped, whisking past the naïve young hostess and out through the doors. Back to the real world in which she could never seem to escape—no matter how hard she tried.

Lee wiped the tears from her cheeks, and bit at her lip to stop any more but the physical pain only seemed to amplify her emotions. She hurried to her car, careful to keep her gaze away from a couple who brushed past her. No one else needed to see her sorrowful display.

The car door slammed. She sank into the driver's seat and rested her cheek against the cold steering wheel. *Focus, Lee. You can do this.* The next tear broke through her weak resolve and splashed onto the black plastic wheel. *I can't even stop myself from crying. How can I continue on like this? I can't even function. I'm so... alone. How will I survive?*

Someone knocked on the window. Her surprised squeal pierced the air inside the car as she jerked back from the wheel.

A little girl stood on the other side of the glass. Her blonde hair was pulled into lop-sided pigtails, and there were smudges of chocolate on the edges of her pudgy candy-pink lips. She was the picture of an angel, and for a moment Lee couldn't find words; she could only stare at the girl.

"Are you all right? Why are you crying?" The girl's muted voice twinkled with innocent concern.

Lee found the window button through her tears and lowered the glass. "I'm okay," she said with a sniff.

"You're crying." The girl ran her fingers down her chubby cheeks. "Don't cry."

The simple command pulled at Lee's heartstrings and she dabbed at her eyes, staunching her tears.

"I'm not crying." Lee gave a thin smile. "Where's your mommy?" She peered out the window, looking for the precious girl's mother but they were the only people in the parking lot. Was the girl an angel sent by Daniel?

"My mommy's an angel," the girl replied, as she played with the end of her right pigtail.

Lee's heart skipped a beat. Maybe she wasn't crazy after all. Maybe Daniel really did send the girl to help her.

"My mommy always told me to make a wish when I am sad," the girl continued. "My wishes always make me happy. Do you want to make a wish?"

The little angel was real.

"Sure, let's make a wish."

The girl smiled. Her childish beauty was a ray of sun. As each second passed between them, Lee's ice-covered heart warmed and surged with joy.

"Okay, close your eyes," the girl said, pinching her face into a squished pucker. Her eye-lashes fluttered and through them there was a gleam of the girl's warm chocolate eyes. "Come on," she urged. "Close your eyes."

Lee obliged, but first peeked once more to see the sweet child's O-shaped mouth and then squeezed her eyes shut. "What should I wish for?"

"Something you want more than anything else."

The joy that flickered to life only moments before, slowed as Lee thought of the one thing she wanted more than anything else, the one thing she'd never have again…Daniel.

"Think of something that makes you happy," the girl said, almost in tune to Lee's thoughts.

Memories of Daniel were the only things left. There had to be more to life— something that wouldn't take his place, but would make her want to live. There had to be something that would make her want to get up in the morning. Something that would fill her with life and make her feel as though she was alive instead of standing in a pool of sinking memories.

Every minute of every day she would love her son. He would always be her first thought in the morning and the last thought at night, but he must have sent this angel to her. He must have wanted her to have more adventures… to start wishing and stop worrying that she might fall.

"Did you make a wish?" The girl asked, her voice like the gentle ringing of bells.

Make a wish.

How simple, yet so hard.

❖Chapter Three❖

Lee tried to make a wish, but she couldn't think of anything she wanted more than Daniel. Maybe someday she could make a wish and have the strength to blindly hope it would come true.

She opened her eyes and smiled at the girl on the other side of the door. Maybe the child wasn't an angel after all. The girl was too imperfect with her chocolate-dotted mouth and lopsided pigtails. It was silly of Lee to consider there was some cosmic force that would come to her in her moment of need.

"Thank you for trying. No more tears, I swear," Lee said, lifting her hand up in an over-the-top vow. "What's your name, sweetheart?"

"Penny. I'm a princess."

Lee gave a small laugh at the sweet child's answer. "Well, Princess Penny, where's your daddy?"

"I'm right here," a man with a deep baritone answered, breaking the spell.

The double glass doors of the restaurant closed behind the broad-shouldered man who carried a plastic bag and wore a familiar grin Lee saw only hours before.

"What are you doing here, Albert? I thought you had someone waiting for you?"

"I did," he said as he stopped beside the girl. The blonde child slipped her starfish fingers inside the man's wind-chapped hand with a familiar ease. "I told you not to run off, Penny. What if you got lost?"

"But I didn't get lost," Penny said, a mischievous smile on her lips. "And this lady was crying. She shouldn't cry."

"I agree, sweetheart. Ms. Lee shouldn't cry." Albert peered over at her. She couldn't help but notice the way his green eyes seemed to hold secrets.

"She and I were making wishes. Do you want to know what I wished for?" Princess Penny asked in less than a breath.

"What did you wish for, honey?" Albert wrapped Penny's fine hair around his strong fingers.

"You know if you tell other people a wish it won't come true." Lee said as her urge to protect, which had lain dormant since Daniel's death, came to life. If there was one thing the girl needed to hold onto, it was the belief that wishes were the key to a door that could only be opened with dreams. If she could save Penny from losing her faith in wishes she could keep dreaming.

"No, that's not true," Penny said, covering her mouth. "I wished that you would come over to our house tomorrow for Christmas. What do you think, Daddy? Can she come?"

An awkward silence filled the winter air between them. Albert opened his mouth, and then shut it as though trying to think of a way out of the uncomfortable position his daughter put him in.

"No," Lee said, as she tried to stop the conversation from bleeding into the ground. "I can't. I have—" She stopped short of the word 'plans.' She didn't want to lie to the girl—or to her father.

Since her divorce, Lee hadn't had plans for Christmas. The last time she'd celebrated had been at her crazy in-law's house or, as Lee dubbed it, the Christmas of non-committal niceties.

That year, her mother-in-law had started her sentences with, "Next year, we should…" and each time the sentence would be left unfinished. Even her in-laws knew she and Jake wouldn't survive another year. There could be no future for them when all they could focus on was their resentment of each other's roles in Daniel's death. The only thing she and Jake had in common was their past. A past couldn't build a future; just a memory.

Something about Penny's unbridled joy and her innocent desire to please, made Lee question her resolve to never celebrate Christmas again. What would it be like to celebrate with the girl and her father? Would there be other family members there? She could imagine the buttery scent of a roasting turkey mixed with the rich, earthy scent of pine. She yearned to have a reason to put aside her anguish and live.

Albert shifted from one foot to another as though putting out a conversational fire his daughter had set. The flames even reached his face, making a thin sheen of sweat on his forehead even though he stood in the lapping winds of a winter evening. She shouldn't intrude on his time with his daughter at Christmas.

"I don't think it's a good idea for—"

"No," Albert interrupted. "We'd really love to have you there, but I gotta warn you I ain't much of a cook."

"It's true," Princess Penny said with a giggle. "He burned my grilled cheese last night."

"Is that right?" She could envision Albert, standing over a skillet with smoke curling up to the ceiling like a beckoning finger.

"We had to eat cold cereal, but it was Lucky Charms and he gave me all his marshmallows."

A marshmallow-giver, the true mark of a great dad. Daniel always wanted his father's marshmallows. Once in a while, Jake gave in, sliding one milk-covered slimy marshmallow onto the edge of Daniel's bowl.

"So what do you think?" Penny asked with her next full breath. "You'll come, won't you?"

The sweat on Albert's forehead was still there, but maybe Lee was wrong in her assumption that he felt uncomfortable with the invitation. Maybe something else made the stoic cowboy uncomfortable—something Lee hadn't seen in a long time; something wonderful.

Lee looked away from Albert's sparkling green eyes. His gaze only made the flux of emotions shift into a dangerous new wave of excitement. And waves always ended up crashing.

"Well, Princess Penny, how many people do you expect for dinner?"

A wide grin wiggled over the girl's face. "Daddy said Santa is coming, so that would make… four!"

Albert twirled Penny's hair. "No, sweetheart, Santa isn't coming for dinner. He only comes when

22

you're asleep…and only if you've been a very good girl this year. Isn't that right, Lee?"

The way he said her name was like candy that melted on his tongue, sweet and savory in its delicate flavor.

"Absolutely," Lee said, finally able to draw her gaze away from Albert's sweet lips. "You have to be a good girl. We'd hate for Santa to put you on the naughty list, wouldn't we?"

Albert glanced at his watch. "And if we don't get home and to bed soon, he might get the wrong idea. It's getting late. So what do you think, Lee? Would you like to come over tomorrow? We'd love to have you."

"How about this?" Lee asked, suddenly all too aware that the moment of stolen happiness would end. "How about I cook dinner and bring it to you?"

"What?" Albert gave her a surprised look. "Are you sure? It's a lot of work." But there seemed to be an undercurrent of relief in his voice. "Just because Penny told you about the cheese sandwich doesn't mean I couldn't figure out how to make… one hell of a mess with a turkey." He gave her a grin that seemed made for his chiseled face.

"I can't guarantee I won't make a mess, but I'll try and cook something you'll enjoy." It didn't matter that she hadn't cooked since before the accident, or she had only a bottle of ketchup and a moldy wedge of cheese in her refrigerator. She would make this a Christmas none of them would ever forget.

❖Chapter Four❖

At nine o'clock on Christmas Eve the parking lot of the one grocery store still open was full of oversized pickup trucks with bumper stickers that read, 'I only wish my wife was this dirty' and 'Love to hunt.' Lee laughed at the collection of husbands. At the door, a man was carrying a baby in a car seat on his arm. His coat was covered with a collection of dried spit and dark bags lay heavy beneath his sleep-deprived eyes. He must have noticed her gaze, as he sent her a half-hearted smile that increased her sympathy for him.

She remembered life with a new baby—days spent in a dazzling whirlwind of feedings, diapers, and an unending supply of questions and insecurities. As a mother, she could look back on those days fondly and remember the sweet smell of Daniel's breath on her skin and the way he reached up to touch her face as they played. As much as she loved the memories, she couldn't forget the sleepless nights or the constant strain that a baby put on a marriage. If she could go back, she would do it all again, but if someone asked her now, as she stared at the last-minute shopper- frazzled new father, she couldn't say she'd want to be a new parent again.

Penny came to mind. The girl said there would only be the three of them at dinner tomorrow. That must mean that Penny and Albert celebrated without the rest of their family. Or did they have more family? Were they alone like her? From the headstone, Lee recalled that Brooke had been gone for more than four years. Penny couldn't be more than six years old.

Had Albert been just like this man? Had he been a widowed father with a baby, stuck in a current of new parent fear? It was no wonder Albert was wrapped around the girl's finger. Penny must be everything to him.

What would it be like to start all over again? To have a child—not a baby, but a young child—in her life?

There wouldn't be diapers and midnight feedings, but there would still be dance classes, swimming lessons, school plays, and teacher conferences. It was easy to imagine herself back in the active role of parenting, driving from place to place with a child. When not busy following the steady flow of activities she could envision them sitting around the table talking about the events of their days. She missed that most of all—those simple moments when the most important thing was each other.

It was around the table where so many of her favorite memories had been made. Daniel had a habit of always leading the discussions with boyish things when he was young, telling stories of boogers and how the girls chased him. As he'd grown, the evenings spent around the table became fewer and fewer, but the stories were still about the females in his life and instead of the events of his school days, his talk turned to his work.

She'd barely noticed those subtle changes when she'd sat around the table with her family. She'd seen the fine lines that accumulated around Jake's eyes and the way his chair moved farther away, but even though she'd seen those small changes she'd not realized how damaging those small actions were. It wasn't until after Daniel died and her ex's chair sat empty that Lee wished she'd moved closer, taken his hand the first night he'd pulled away, instead of resenting him for his actions.

Resentment brought her nothing but bitterness, an empty house, and a lonely heart.

As lonely as she may have been, it was impossible to replace her family. But it would be fun to have a child around; a girl who could help her to remember a brighter side to life. Daniel had been such a fun baby, but she'd never had a little girl. Her ex had been convinced adding another child to their family was too much. "We're a threesome. Life's good. Why go around messing with things, when we're happy?" He used to say.

Lee gave in to his wishes, not wanting to create discord. He'd been right. They had been happy. Life had been easy. She'd tried so hard to be the perfect wife, mother... but failed. It was hard to think it wouldn't happen again. It was easy to daydream about another life, but it could only be just that—a daydream. No one ever got a chance to go back and fix the mistakes they made in the past. There was only one choice—keep moving.

The cart jingled as she made her way around the store. Luck was on her side as she grabbed the last can of pumpkin for a pie and a misplaced can of black olives for the table. Penny would love the olives, pushing them down on her fingers and pretending she was an alien. The meat department was straight ahead and it was surprisingly quiet. The men who'd swarmed around the clothing and knickknack aisles had disappeared, leaving only her and her quest for the centerpiece and most important item of the Christmas table—the turkey.

She walked down an aisle filled with the rich aroma of breads and to the display of open freezers. Wheeling her cart to the edge of the freezer section, she peered into the empty steel-racked chasm. It was the same as she walked farther down the section. *Turkey. Turkey. Turkey.* And the guts of the refrigerated section lay barren.

Okay. No turkey. She sighed. *Maybe ham.*

There were the same jeering signs when she arrived at the ham area in the meat department. *Ham. Ham. Ham.* Once again, the section lay empty; completely devoid of anything that even resembled the traditional Christmas mainstays.

The refrigerated hum of the empty boxes only added insult to injury as Lee moved down the aisle. Even the chickens were gone. As were the Cornish game hens. The only thing left was one large salmon, whose glassy black-centered eyeball seemed to watch her as she approached. She'd never been one for fish, but the only other meat that seemed to be around was a display of hot dogs stacked into a triangle of meat.

Nothing said Christmas more than a weenie on a platter. No, the salmon would have to do.

****

It had been such a long time since she'd cooked, it was as though she'd just run a mile after too long on the couch. Her fingers ached from the potato peeler and her ankles were swollen from standing too long behind the sink, but she was bound and determined to make this

Christmas a success. To celebrate again was a gift. It wasn't the first time she'd been invited to someone's home for the holiday since Daniel's death, but it was the first time she'd *wanted* to go.

True, the invitation hadn't been all Albert's doing, but it still excited her to be part of part of a happy little family—if only for a day.

On the couch were four presents—two perfectly wrapped boxes for Penny and two for Albert. She'd taken her time and picked out the prettiest paper with pink princesses and snowflakes for Penny and timeless blue and silver paper for Albert. She didn't know what to get them, but she'd had fun searching the store for its hidden treasures.

The oven timer went off. The salmon was done. She pulled it out of the oven and covered it in a towel. Loading all the food and presents into her car, she made her way across Missoula to a small house on Beckwith. Lugging the gifts under her arm, she rang the doorbell and waited.

Penny's shrill squeal filled the air as the door swung open. "You're here! You're here!" Penny shouted. "Daddy, she's here!"

It had been a long time since she'd been met with a warmer welcome. Penny saw the princess wrapping paper and her face went from bright to glow-in-the-dark. "Is that for me?"

"Well, let's see…" Lee teased. "Have you been a good girl all year?"

Penny nodded, making her sweet golden curls bounce to life. "Can I open it now, or do I have to wait until after we eat?"

"After we eat," Albert said as he walked down the hallway to the front door. He wore a red and white checkered apron and held a wet rag in his hand.

"That's a fabulous apron," Lee said, releasing the presents into Penny's excited grip. "Do you have one for me?"

"I didn't think…" Albert glanced down and his tanned face turned a muddled shade of red. "Ah, shit." He pulled the end of the tie and lifted the unforgettable apron away, exposing a full suit. The black lapels were slightly too wide and the buttons stretched a little too tight across his stomach. He folded the apron over his arm.

"I happen to think that is a fine apron. But I'm glad you took it off. It's not every day I get the chance to see a man in a full suit. You look great."

Albert swelled with pride. "I couldn't go all the way *city*. I had to keep the cowboy boots." He stuck out his foot, showing the shining black leather of a freshly polished boot. He stepped beside her and leaning down, he whispered into her ear, "The only time I ever went to this much trouble before, was on my wedding day."

Her body warmed with the sudden flood of sensations that arose as his warm breath brushed against her ear and caressed her neck. "Thank you," she said, staring down at the simple white top and knee-length black skirt she'd wrestled from the back of her closet just for today.

She tried to not notice how he seemed to take in her scent, or the way his eyes seemed to widen as he looked at her. They were nothing more than single-serving friends who'd met in an unfortunate circumstance, and only came together because of the wishes of a child. They each had their own lives and, even though they'd spend this holiday together, as soon as it was over they would simply go back to life as it had been before, perhaps sharing an occasional phone call or a quick acknowledgement as they passed each other on the street.

"I need to get the food out of the car," she said, trying to create a comfortable emotional distance between herself and the too-handsome cowboy.

"Let me give you a hand." He stepped back and his eyes dimmed, as if he guessed her intention. "Wait here, Penny," he said, but Penny was busy in the living room with the presents.

He followed Lee to the car, and she could sense his eyes upon her, caressing her just as his breath had earlier. As much as she didn't want to like the attention, she couldn't control the sudden desire that coursed through her like oxygen, filling each cell of her body with a desperate need for him to be near her again. She needed his touch and his rich scent—a subtle combination of aftershave mixed with a hint of cinnamon—brush over her.

When she reached into the trunk, she could sense his closeness. The warmth of his body radiated in the cold winter morning like steam rising from earth frozen for too long and finally came back to life in the spring sunshine.

"Here, take the fish." She handed him the black roaster with the salmon inside.

"Fish?"

"You don't like fish, do you?" She grabbed a bag filled to the top with bread, cranberry sauce, a green salad, and enough vegetables for twenty people.

He gave her a guilty smile. "I'm sure anything you cook will be amazing—and far better than anything I could've made. Before we met, I was going to really go out of my way and microwave some chicken nuggets for me and Penny. Anything has to be better than dinosaur-shaped chicken nuggets for Christmas dinner."

Lee smiled as she thought of sitting around the Christmas dinner table their plates full of little dinosaurs. "Unfortunately, fish is a far cry from chicken nuggets. I hope Penny will eat it. I know kids aren't huge fish fans normally, but there wasn't much choice at the store."

"Ah, she'll love it—just like I'm sure I will. Thank you for doing this for us. It means a lot." He gave her a nod before he turned and moved toward the house.

She followed him in. Penny sat next to the tree with a pink package in her hands—no doubt imagining what hidden treasure lay beneath its enticing paper.

Their living room was small and the only Christmas decoration was a tree whose sparse limbs were covered in strings of popcorn and construction paper rings. What few glass ornaments adorned its branches were of princesses and tiny white baby shoes. There were no antique glass bulbs or family heirlooms. It was almost as if Albert's life began with Penny. The ornaments reminded her of her own life, clearly defined into two parts—before Daniel's death and after.

Albert must have felt the same division after the loss of his wife. Evidence of his feelings was evident, from the tree to the few pictures that adorned the walls. But unlike Lee's house, which stood as a shrine to her son, it was as if Albert stripped his home of anything that would make him relive the pain of losing Brooke. Undoubtedly, he must feel the same pain that seemed to be reawakened by the unexpected simple things—a bird on a branch, a certain song on the radio, or the way someone's smile could make the very cells of her being ache.

"Your tree is beautiful." Lee ran her fingers over the course red construction paper ring as she thought of the laughter and joy that must have gone into the chain's making.

"Isn't it pretty?" Penny looked up from her treasure. "Daddy made the popcorn string, but I helped with the rings. Can you believe he didn't know how to make them? I had to teach him," she said with pride.

"Was he a good student?" Lee smiled at Albert who gave her a quick wink.

Penny shrugged. "All right, I guess. He kept wanting to make them red, red, green, but after a while he got it right."

"Men," Lee said with a laugh. "It's a good thing they have us around, huh? They just have no sense of what looks good."

Penny giggled as Lee followed Albert into the kitchen.

In the small square room there was a toaster, a run-of-the-mill microwave, and a package of shortbread cookies on the counter.

"Just so you know, I think I know what looks good," Albert said with an appreciative nod.

A faint warmth rose in Lee's cheeks. "Thank you," she mumbled as she sat down her bag and fumbled around, taking out its contents and laying them on the pristine white counters.

Albert sat the roaster down on the stove and lifted the lid. "Um, Lee? Is it supposed to be like this?" He stared at the contents of the pan.

"What do you mean?" She moved over beside him.

"You know... Is it supposed to be *cold*?"

The silver fish was carefully stuffed with lemon slices, bits of fresh herbs, and slabs of butter. Yellow smooth, unmelted butter.

It couldn't be cold. It hadn't been a long drive across town from her house. She remembered it as clear as day. She'd taken the bags out to the car, come back, opened the oven, pulled out the fish, and carried it to the car.

As she recalled, she hadn't even felt the eyelash-curling heat of the oven when she'd retrieved the main dish. And it hadn't been warm on her hands when she'd carried it out. How could she not notice?

"Okay," she said in a sigh. "Where's your oven? We'll slip it in. Fish doesn't take that long to cook. It'll be ready in a jiff. Maybe we can open presents first, then eat."

Albert sat the lid of the roaster down and turned to face her. "That would be great, but my oven doesn't work. I've been meaning to get it fixed for a while now, but it's just something Penny and I don't use very often."

She couldn't blame him for not getting his oven fixed. She'd rarely used hers in the last few years. So little in fact, she must have forgotten how to turn it on.

"Okay," she said with a smile. "No biggie. We'll just fry it up."

Albert gave an uncomfortable cough. "Yeah, it's not just the oven that's broken—it's the whole stove."

Why did this have to happen when she was trying to make a good impression?

I can't get a lucky break, she thought for a moment and then stopped. It wasn't true. She had gotten lucky. She wasn't alone. She wasn't the party of one she had been just last night. Who cared about some fish?

Around the small white, nearly untouched kitchen was a dishwasher. "How about your dishwasher? Does it work?"

"Like a charm. But what does my dishwasher have to do with cooking dinner?"

"Well, if we can't bake the fish or fry the fish, we'll have to steam it." She gave a prideful smile.

"You sure know how to make lemons into lemonade, don't you?" He gave her a charming grin. Before she could move away, he reached up and pushed a wayward hair out of her face and behind her ear, his fingers grazing her skin. She went still and the desire she'd tried to escape at the car returned with a new strength.

Grabbing a roll of tinfoil out of the paper bag, she pulled out a sheet and spread the fish onto the thin aluminum. "I haven't done this before, but I saw the recipe on Pinterest and it didn't seem too hard. I think I only have to put the fish in foil, add spices, and steam. Easy." After she'd folded the tinfoil over and crimped the edges, she slid the fish onto the top rack of the empty dishwasher. "Nothing to it, right?"

"If you say so," Albert said, his lips pulled into a sexy half-grin. "I'm always up for a new adventure."

"Well, if there's one thing I can guarantee, it's that if you're around me enough, there's always an adventure."

"Then I will make sure to stick around."

Her stomach clenched with excitement. "I hope so." She flexed her rusty charm and sent him a wilted smile. "Why don't we open up presents and then we can eat?"

"I know Penny will be happy to hear that. She's been playing with the gifts all morning."

In the living room, Penny had constructed a pyramid out of the pink and red packages. "Are you guys ready?"

"Go ahead, sweetheart. Why don't you start unwrapping the presents?"

Penny tore through the paper, her face lighting up as she opened up the gifts from Albert. There were dolls and dresses, beads, and clay—everything a girl could ever want.

The pyramid of gifts grew smaller and smaller until the last two gifts were the ones Lee brought. It was silly, but Lee couldn't help the excitement and nervousness she felt. It was true that it was better to give than to receive. It was the best feeling in the world to see the joy in Penny's face after she opened a gift.

Penny picked up the gift Lee brought and gave the doll-filled box a squeeze. Instead of opening the gift, she held the present in her arms.

"Aren't you going to open it?" Albert asked, holding a stuffed dog in his weathered hands.

Penny shook her head.

"Why not?"

Penny looked over at her and smiled. "Ms. Lee already gave me the present I wanted most of all."

"Huh?" Albert frowned. "Did she let you open up a present when I wasn't looking?"

"No…" Penny hugged the gift in her arms closer. "She made you happy."

❖Chapter Five❖

The scents of lemon and warm fish rose from the dishwasher as it beeped, letting them know the cycle ended.

The bell tones of Penny's voice echoed into the kitchen as Albert walked in. "Is dinner ready?"

"I hope so," Lee said as she silently prayed that nothing went wrong.

Lee opened the dishwasher's door. A billow of steam spilled out, obscuring the tinfoil that sat on the top rack. Cracking open the door farther, globs of pink mush came into view. Bits of pink splashed around the aluminum box as if someone had thrown bits of fish confetti around the washer.

Lee slapped her hands over her mouth as she gasped. "Oh my God!"

"What happened? The fish isn't still cold, is it?"

"No…" Lee stared in at the tinfoil that she'd neatly folded around the fish, but now was bulbous and leaking water and little bits of fish. "I screwed it up." She opened the rack as water splashed down from what had once been the well-intentioned main course. "I can't believe it."

"It's okay. Don't worry." He put his hand on her shoulder and spun her around. "I don't care about any damn fish."

"I'm sorry about the mess." She motioned to the fish-filled washer. "I can't do anything right."

"I don't care about the mess—it will all be part of the memory. And there are plenty of things you do right. You tried, damn it… and that's more than I can say for most."

"But there's nothing to eat…"

"We'll figure it out. Don't worry." He dropped his hand from her shoulder down to her waist and the sudden action made her frustration slip away, leaving only her embarrassment. "And just think, we'll never forget this—our first ill-fated Christmas fish." He pulled her into his arms. The warm scent of his cologne sat fresh on his shirt, but it didn't completely mask his scent. "Or this." He leaned down and took her lips with his, his touch tender.

Her lips felt numb, but the rest of her body came alive with the feel of his kiss.

He eased back from her lips and she could sense his smile.

"Thank you, Albert. Thank you…for everything."

"You're the one that deserves thanks." He rested his forehead against hers and his warm breath brushed against her cheeks. "I've tried to make Christmas great for Penny ever since Brooke's passing, but it's just been me and Penny every year. No matter how much we decorate or how much we pretend it's a celebration, it hasn't felt like Christmas. For the first time in a long time it feels like Christmas again." He paused for a second. "And I know this may sound crazy, but it's like you were meant to be here. We were meant to be. It's almost like Brooke wanted us to come together."

Lee's mind went to the moment she'd first seen Penny. She'd thought the girl was an angel sent by Daniel. Looking back, it was hard to discount the possibility that she'd been right. And maybe Albert was right; maybe Brooke had a hand in their meeting as well. "That's not crazy at all."

She pressed the side of her face against his chest and danced in the musical beat of his heart.

"Lee?"

"Hmm?"

"What do you wish for?"

There were many things that came to mind—to be in his arms, hear Penny's laughter, start a family. But even more than that, she wished for love.

"Remember, if you say a wish out loud it won't come true." She smiled against his chest.

"I don't believe it…"

"I don't want to risk not getting my wish."

Penny walked into the kitchen and smiled. She'd caught them. "Daddy?"

Lee wiggled free of his arms.

"Yes, honey?"

"Can I have a piece of pie?"

Albert glanced down at the mess of fish that smeared the dishwasher. "Sure, why don't we have dessert?"

Walking to the fridge, he opened the door and pulled out a green box. He opened the box and drew out a pie covered in clouds of whipped cream and chocolate shavings.

"Is that French Silk?" Lee asked.

"Yep. I got it at the restaurant last night. They were just bringing it out of the back, as though it was waiting for me when I walked in," Albert said. "It's funny, I didn't know what I wanted until I saw it, but just like you, it's just what I needed." He smiled.

His words echoed through her heart. Any question that Daniel had a role in their meeting, disappeared. He was the reason she, Albert, and Penny met. Daniel wanted her to move forward.

Albert opened the sides of the box and the pie slid out. Its aluminum dish teetered on the edge of the counter. "Watch out! It's going to fall!" Lee reached out instinctively to grab the pie.

Before she could reach the pie, Albert grabbed the pan and slid it back to safety. Lee stopped. Her arms were extended in front of her and, as she moved to lower them, Albert took her hands. "Lee?"

"What?" She couldn't stop staring at the lovely white clouds on the top of the pie.

"It's okay."

"No. It's not okay... I can't fall."

"*You* can't fall?"

She glanced up at him as she realized what she had said "I meant *it*... the pie."

He looked at her sideways as he squeezed her hands. "I hope you know that if you fall. I'll be there to catch you."

His words filled her hollowness and made her breath stick in her throat. How could he know the words she so desperately needed to hear?

"It's okay, Ms. Lee," Penny said, "Daddy's a good catch."

Albert's laughter mixed with hers. Penny was right; he was a catch.

"You know what, Penny?" Lee reached over and laced her fingers through Penny's bobbed curls.

"What?"

"I think I'm just like you."

"Really?" Penny smiled as she dipped her finger into the pie's fluffy cream. "Why?" She popped her finger into her mouth.

"I think I already got my wish."

She caught Albert's gaze and sank into the promises that were held in his spring green eyes; promises of safety, a future, and a life she thought she'd never have again.

Albert rubbed his finger over the back of her other hand. "And what was it that you wished for?"

"I wished for love."

CENTRAL BARK AT CHRISTMAS

JENNIFER CONNER

❖Chapter One❖

"You can keep the dog."

Tennyson Adams struggled to pull Mobley's collar as the dog tried to wiggle free of her grasp and out the door. "I don't understand...what?" she asked, stunned by James's words.

The distant, cool look in his eyes said a lot. She'd never seen this side of James. Had he saved it for a moment like now? Did this detachment make him a better lawyer? They'd lived together for the past four months, and at this moment he looked at her as though she was a stranger. His face was a mask that she couldn't read. He didn't look angry or sad ; there were no emotions. Her heart thudded so loud it echoed in her ears.

"The dog is the only thing I can remember that we bought with *your* money. I wouldn't have got a mutt. As I said, you can keep the dog. You know that *I* bought everything else in this apartment— the furniture, the appliances, and most of your clothes."

"That's not true! "

"Well, I didn't buy *that*." He snorted in disgust and waved his hand in her direction. "That's your waitress uniform. After you get the dog in your car, I took the time to pack your things in shopping bags. Take them with you I don't really want you to come back when Rachel's here, and she doesn't want to see you either."

"Rachel?" Tennyson blinked. "As in my friend from

high- school, Rachel?" She felt bile rise in her throat and thought she'd be sick. She drew in a deep breath to keep her stomach in place. "How long has this affair been going on?" Her hand shook when she pulled the leather strap of her purse back up on her shoulders.

"It doesn't matter now. A while. Rachel and I plan to get married."

All Tennyson could do was nod. Her mouth felt too dry to speak. James never wanted to commit to say they "lived together" much less even hint about marriage. She tipped her chin high. Her mother raised three daughters as a single mom. If she taught her girls anything it was, "hold your head high. If a man doesn't want you, you don't grovel." Second choice would never work, she deserved better than that. She deserved better than James.

Tennyson led Mobley to her car and guided the key into the lock. The dog patiently waited, knowing the routine, as she slid the worn wool blanket over the front seat before he jumped in. The first raindrop hit her forehead. In a few seconds it turned into a cloudburst.

Rain dribbled down her face and soaked her clothes. She'd forgotten her coat at the restaurant. Looking up at the light in the second story window, she wondered if Rachel was there. How could her friend betray her? The sky lit brilliant white with a crack of lighting that pulled her away from her thoughts.

By the time Tennyson returned to the front, her bags were out on the steps.

James was right. There wasn't much in this house that was hers. It was all his. She didn't want any of it anyway. He'd even returned her heart in a matter of seconds and it was probably at the bottom of one of the reusable shopping bags.

"Oh, no…" She mumbled to herself. She grabbed for the first bag. "Please let it be here." She rummaged through the clothes. "Damn," she said as she went through the last bag. Tennyson's great-grandmothers porcelain box wasn't there. It was the only thing in the house she cared about. She looked at the doorbell and bit her lip. She couldn't face him again. Not right now. She'd come back for the box in the next few days.

She trudged back to the car and threw the rest of her belongings in the back and then slid in. Grasping the wheel, her vision blurred with tears. Mobley, panting and wagging his tail gave her a wet and sloppy kiss that ran up her cheek to her ear.

Tennyson sniffed back tears and scratched the brown scruffy fur behind the dog's ears. "I got the better end of the deal—James is a bastard, jerk, an asshat…" her words trailed off as Mobley gave her another lick.

She pulled her phone from her purse. She looked at the photo of her and Rachel smiling with their arms around each other's shoulders, and pressed *Delete*. Then she found James, followed suit and dropped her phone back into her purse. She didn't need anyone, at least not a *human*. All she needed was Mobley. He'd always be there. He'd never let her down.

Tennyson backed out of the parking space and headed out into the city. Even though she desperately wanted to look in the rearview mirror, she kept her eyes trained on the road. When she got around the corner, she pulled into an empty lot. Tennyson screamed and hit the steering wheel. Heartbreak and betrayal ate away her resolve, and she cried until there was nothing left.

Six months later…

"Hey Shel," Tennyson said as she grabbed the leash off the hook on the wall. "I've got a few hours before my shift at the restaurant begins. I'm going to take Mobley to the dog park before it gets too crowded and they're predicting a storm for later today."

Shelly popped her head around the corner and pulled out an earbud. "I'll be home late tonight, so leave the light on."

"Sure. I have an extra shift too, so you might beat me." If someone told Tennyson that her life would work out okay without James, she never would have believed them. But now, it was water under the bridge. She'd found an apartment with a girl from work, and her mom loaned her a few hundred dollars to buy necessities like new sheets and bath towels. Tennyson picked up all the extra shifts at work and even though she usually felt tired, she'd made enough to pay her mom back and keep a little on the side.

Tennyson looked around her small apartment and smiled. She and Shelly had picked out their odd mix of Goodwill furnishings together and even managed to get a hand-me-down fake Christmas tree, complete with bubble lights and ornaments her mom gave her.

She liked shopping at thrift stores. It was the 'cool' thing to do now. She wondered if James got the memo? She liked the bright orange and green color scheme mixed in with the tacky red and green holiday decor. This place felt like home. Hers. At James's house everything was decorated in black and silver. Black wasn't a color. Black was the non-existence of color. Recently, she'd noticed there was a new spring to her step and renewed energy when she woke up. Mobley was at the foot of her bed every morning and that helped her through the times when she felt lonely. Though he was a big bed hog, it was nice to wake up with his furry face looking back.

Her plan was working. Stick to the furry companions and all would be well.

Tennyson parked her car and unlocked the back doors. Mobley knew they'd arrived at the dog park. He jumped and barked in the back seat. She grabbed the leash, and as soon as she opened the back door, he leaped out and ran toward the high chain-link gate. When she opened the first gate, Mobley bounded past her and pawed the ground until she opened the inner gate to the park. Then he rushed past.

She was surprised that there weren't more dogs at the park that day. Even though it felt cold, it wasn't raining. A breeze ruffled her hair and she pulled her coat closed at the neck. Tennyson followed Mobley to the clearing under the trees, then sat on the wooden bench, and stretched her legs out.

"Good morning," a deep voice said. When she jumped in shock, the thirty-something man smiled. "Sorry, I didn't mean to startle you. I thought you'd have heard me on the gravel."

"Out for a jog?" Tennyson gave him the once-over. Navy blue shorts hugged lean hips. She tried not to ogle his bare, broad shoulders and chest damp with perspiration. The brown skin of his biceps were dusted with curly black hair. It was the middle of winter and way too cold to go out without a shirt… but still. .

"I come here before work. I can run and my crazy dog can let out some of his pent up energy." He gave her an easy smile that put a small dimple in his left cheek. His hair was jet-black and his dark, velvety eyes were the same shade as his hair, nearly black. He looked like one of the sexy leading men from the Bollywood movies she'd been addicted to a few years back. He wiped his forehead with the back of his forearm. "I haven't seen you here before."

"Mobley is my dog, he's over there." She pointed. "He loves it here and would be the official dog park greeter if there was such a position. I come on most days but I work different shifts, so we bounce around."

"Shift work can be hard when it changes." He stretched his calf. "Where do you work?"

"I'm a manager at *The Neighborhood Grill*."

He looked up. "No kidding. I love that place! Their turkey grilled sandwich with avocado is addictive." He took a step closer and stuck out his hand. "The name's Par."

"Your parents are golfers?"

He thought for a second and then laughed. "I've never heard anyone say that. That's funny." As he grasped her wrist, she noticed his skin was a rich, chocolate color against the paleness of hers.

"I assume your name's short for something else?" Heat flooded her cheeks as she dropped his hand and stepped back.

"Parkash. What about you? Do you have a name that I can put with Mobley?"

"Let's keep it at dog park etiquette and casual." Too much too soon. Arms length.

"Sure." Three dogs came barreling around the corner. Par grabbed the tree to keep his balance as one of them brushed past him. "Hey, watch it, you hoodlums." He pointed. "Mine's the instigator with the red bandana around her neck. Her name's Boci. She's a puggle. Part pug, part beagle. I got her from a rescue about six months ago." His dog squealed to a stop almost stumbling over herself. Par bent and scratched behind her ears.

"She's adorable."

"Yeah, she's my girl… for right now anyway." He shot her a sexy look and then a grin.

Her stomach did a little flip. The chemistry snapped between them, but Tennyson quickly tamped it down. The three dogs ran off in the other direction.

He stood, straightened his back and frowned. "The other dog who's running with ours, I wonder where his owner is? I only saw two cars out in the lot."

She shrugged. "I don't know. If they left, I'm sure they will be back soon." She grabbed the leash and headed toward the main gate. "It was nice meeting you, Par."

"Likewise."

She felt his gaze on her back as she walked away. She started to put a little swing in her hips, but stopped. She gave herself a mental tap. She reminded herself, no men. But he was awfully cute. James was blond. She'd never been attracted to anyone with dark skin and black hair, but with Par she could make an exception. But again... he didn't have ears or four legs... so definitely no, it didn't matter how cute he was.

She whistled with two fingers, waited for Mobley and then took him out to the parking lot. Tennyson looked over the field and caught one last look at Par as he played with the two remaining dogs. He threw a tennis ball and they both ran after it. He laughed. He'd put on his sweatshirt... *too bad.*

When she and Mobley got in the car, she looked at the clock on the dashboard. 9:45. She was off tomorrow morning at this same time, and Mobley seemed to get along with Boci and the other dog. Mobley liked to have a playmate. She'd finished all of her holiday shopping , so she had a little extra time. She might have to try and make it back here... for Mobley's sake.

❖Chapter Two❖

Par looked at the clock that sat on the corner of his desk and then at the stack of files. He'd come in at five to get a jump on the day, but no matter how early he arrived, it didn't seem to matter. The more he worked in his father's corporate land trust company the more he hated going to work. This was his father's company not his.

His father told him that if he worked alongside his brother, he promised that Par would be placed in charge of the company's foundation. But it had been three years and it still hadn't happened. He loved his parents, and owed them much. But since his family moved here from India when he was a child, all his father did was work. Status climbing was the last thing *he* cared about. He cared much more about mountain climbing.

He pushed away from the desk and crossed his arms over his chest. He was smart and his college education trained him for this profession, but he couldn't keep his head in the game. He finished his protein drink, stood and walked to the executive restrooms where he quickly changed into his jogging outfit. If he timed it well, he could be out the door before the front desk people arrived and not be swamped with more work.

Par knew he deserved breaks like everyone else, though his father disagreed about taking any time off.

He took the back four stories of stairs, and headed

out into the alley. He'd take an extra minute to swing by his house and pick up Boci. As he hit his stride, he wondered if the cute girl he'd seen the other day might be there again.

That just might make the morning doable.

As he jogged into the parking lot, he noticed the girl's red car took up two slots. He smiled. *She's cute, but she can't park worth a darn.*

Par grabbed Boci's leash and opened the gates. He'd take a quick half-loop through the park to make it look as though he'd stumbled upon her again. He clicked his tongue and Boci trotted up alongside him. He broke through the trees. This time she faced him so he didn't have to worry about startling her.

"Hey," he said. "Fancy meeting you here again. We have to stop meeting like this; the dogs will talk."

"Good morning." She smiled and flipped her shoulder-length brown hair out of the collar of her coat as she buttoned it closed. "How's your morning going?"

"Not great, until I came here."

"You had a bad morning on your way to work?"

"On the way to? No. I've already been there almost four hours."

"Workaholic, huh?"

"That would not be a word that I'd use to describe myself." He picked up a milk jug filled with water and dumped it into the bowl.

"Where do you work?"

"My dad owns Cascade Land Trust. I work there." He watched her gaze drop and she took a step back. "Do you know someone who works there?"

"Well, not really *works* there, My ex is one of the lawyers who represents your firm."

"Just for the record, I have nothing to do with the lawyers. You said ex? That's nice to know."

She grinned. "I guess I can laugh about it now. That's a good thing right. I just remember him mentioning Cascade Trust. My name's Tennyson. You asked me yesterday, but I didn't tell you. I felt like kind of a jerk, it was a simple friendly question."

"Nice to meet you Tennyson. My parents like golf and yours were hoping for a boy that played racket sports."

She laughed. It made her brown eyes sparkle and his mouth felt a little dry. He'd had his share of girlfriends in the past, but it had been months since he'd even been out on a date. All work and no play. Just what his father wanted. *I should ask her out on a date.* "Hey, what're you—"

"Mobley!" she shouted. "Be careful, you're going to hurt Boci if you play that hard." She stopped and watched the three dogs run down the hill. "That other dog is still here. I don't see anyone again and I'm starting to worry."

Par looked around. "You're right. This is the second day. Do you think he's been here alone since yesterday?"

"The park keeper would have seen him."

He shook his head. "Not necessarily. I'm sure the park attendant comes at closing and takes a quick look around. If there are no cars, they assume all the dogs are gone. It's twenty acres."

"A dog could get lost. Out by the main gate, there's

a number to call in case of emergencies."

Par followed Tennyson and listed while she dialed the number listed by the front gate and explained the issue. Her brows were knit into a frown as she replied to the voice on the other end of the line, "That's okay. I'll take care of it." She ended the call and dropped her phone back in her purse.

"What did they say?"

"He said that they would send the Animal Control out. I don't like that idea. Poor guy. There's water but he's had no food for a few days. How could someone do that? Just leave their dog?"

"Not everyone in the world is nice." When the three dogs made another run past them, he stepped in front of the last dog to stop it. Bending down, he looked at the tag on his collar. "Duke. There isn't a contact phone number, but at least we have his name."

Tennyson reached into her purse. "Here boy," she called as she unwrapped her sandwich. The dog quickly came to her. She held the bread out to him. He ate it in one gulp and wagged his tail. "I had a Lab when I was a kid. Duke's black, I had a Golden, but they are super sweet dogs." She looked up at him. "What should we do? I can't take him back to my place; it's super small and my roommate has just come to terms with Mobley. She says she's a cat person."

"The park owner mentioned the—"

"No," she stated solidly. "They can't take him there. He's scared, cold and hungry." She bit her lip in concentration, obviously trying to think of an alternative.

"I can take him"

"You can?" She stood and brushed off her hands. Her face brightened. "That would be great. I can make flyers and maybe his owners will come back for him." She dug back in her purse. "Damn, I left my phone with a camera at home."

"Do you have a piece of paper and a pen?" He motioned to his shorts and t-shirt. "I don't carry much on me when I run."

"Sure." She pulled out a green metal case, and then handed it to him.

"This is my address. Why don't you come by around seven and you can take a picture of him for the flyers. We can design and print the flyers there; I have lots of ink and paper. Could I also interest you in dinner?"

She paused for a long moment, and then said, "Sure. Today's my day off so my evening's open."

He glanced at his watch. "I better get back to work. You wouldn't by any chance have a spare leash in your car. I have to get them both back to my house and I'm not sure how well Duke follows orders."

She held the leash out to him. "Here, take mine. I only have to get Mobley back to my car."

Par stepped closer and put a hand on her arm. She looked down at his hand before she met his gaze. He wanted to touch her cheek to see if her skin was as soft as it looked. "Duke will be fine. We'll take care of him, so don't worry."

"I'm not worried… now."

Touch her cheek, hell, what he really wanted to do was kiss her. It was such a nice treat to meet a woman who was more interested in another living thing than if her purse matched her shoes. He reluctantly dropped his hand and hooked the leash onto the silver hook on Duke's collar. "Come on guys," he said to the dogs. As he jogged away, he turned back and said over his shoulder. "See you at seven."

"Can I bring Mobley, or would that be too much?"

"No, sure bring him. I have a big house."

The dogs were the least of his problem. He'd offered to make Tennyson diner. Good God, he was the world's worst cook. What was he thinking? Now, what would he do?

❖Chapter Three❖

Tennyson pushed the remaining hangers to one side and peered into her closet. There was a pile of clothes strewn across the bed and more that fell onto the floor. Mobley watched her with intense interest.

She held up a grey sweater dress in one hand and a red one in the other and then asked him, "Which do you like?"

He wagged his tail and then scratched his ear with his back leg.

"I thought you said you swore off guys," Shelly asked with her hip propped against the doorframe.

"I did."

"I call bull." Shelly came into the room, pushed the clothes to one side, and then flopped onto the bed. "I know you're off work today, and you just sorted your closet by color last week, so that means you have a date."

"It's not a date. I met this guy at the dog park—"

"So it *is* a guy." Shelly rolled to her stomach and braced her chin with her hands. "Come on… more juicy details. Is he cute?"

Tennyson paused before she answered, "Yes, he's cute, but that's not the point, the point is this isn't a date."

"So why all the fuss then? I still call bull."

"I'm just going over to his place for dinner and to help make flyers. We found this lost dog, well more like abandoned dog. Par offered to take him in until we found a more permanent solution or his owner has a reality check and takes him back."

"One dog's enough, you can't bring him here."

Tennyson rolled her eyes. "I know! That's why *he* took the dog."

"So you're going over there to this guy's house to make flyers, hang out and eat his food, but it's not a date."

Tennyson started to speak but then snapped her mouth closed. The thought crossed her mind that tonight could be considered a date. It wasn't a *terrible* notion. That was if she ever could make up her mind on what to wear. She'd been on tons of dates, but this was a "dog date". She had no idea what that entailed.

She held a white T-shirt over her favorite pair of jeans on the bed. The look said casual but with a deep enough vee in the shirt that it would show a little cleavage.

Shelly grinned. "That's your boob shirt. I knew this was a date."

Tennyson shook her head and dropped the shirt on the bed. "Sometimes I wonder why you're my friend."

"Cause ya love me." Shelly stood and gave her a hug. "I was starting to worry about you. It's been six months. I thought you might join a nunnery."

"Not quite. Unless it's the Julie Andrews kind in *The Sound of Music* and I end up with Christopher Plummer."

"You're taking Mobley, right? So if this Par guy turns out to be a jerk Mobley could bite him."

"I don't think that will be necessary. I can handle myself just fine." She laughed as she scooped up her clothes and headed for the shower. "If he turns out like James, I'll bite him myself."

"That could add some extra fun to the 'date.'" Shelly called out.

Tennyson closed the bathroom door and turned on the hot water.

****

Par scrambled around the main floor of his house and frantically picked things up. He'd gotten held up at work, like most nights, and now it was fifteen minutes until he told Tennyson to be here and the place was a mess. Pizza box. Empty beer bottle. *Man, who lives here?, It can't be me.* Spending his precious time off at the warehouse, he'd come home exhausted most nights. Take out, a beer and watch an international soccer match was all he could get his head wrapped around before he fell asleep.

Par made a mental note to himself that if she wore a coat, he shouldn't hang it in the front closet. He'd stuffed his gym bag and three pairs of tennis shoes inside, and the closet no longer smelled like a bed of roses.

Par grabbed a clean cloth out of the drawer, he scooped up cleaner and wiped down the counters. He was also a coffee grounds pig. Like everyone else, he should just buy coffee in the morning and avoid all this mess of making it himself to save a few dollars.

When he'd arrived home he noticed a cushion in the living room chewed to shreds. Par would worry about that in a few minutes. There was a knock on the door. He peeked through the hole and let out a sigh of relief. He swung open the door.

"Hi Mom." He kissed her cheek and took the tray from her hand.

"So, who is this girl that you are having over?"

"We found an abandoned dog." As if on cue Duke and Boci ran into the living room. "She's coming over to make flyers and maybe we can try and convince his owner to take him back."

His mother raised an eyebrow. "Is she a nice *Indian* girl?"

"No, just a nice girl. Come on Mom, give me a break. You and dad have to figure out what you want. Dad wants me to work all the time, and you want me to date. There are no Indian girls at the office. And besides this isn't a date."

"You are not from the old country, I know that. So, I'm pleased that you are spending time with someone. I was so happy that you asked me to cook." She pulled her pink sarong higher and then frowned. "Do you think that it will be too spicy? Some American girls don't like spicy."

"I don't know enough about her to know what she likes and doesn't like. But she'd be crazy not to like your Butter Chicken and *Baigan Bharta*." Par put an arm around her and hugged.

"You're right." Her eyes filled with pride from his compliment. She looked around. "Would you like me to help you clean up your place before she gets here?"

"No, thanks. It's good enough. I'll talk to you tomorrow." He took her arm and guided her out the door. When she started her car and drove off, he waved from the porch. He hurried back into the kitchen. Grabbing the clay baker she'd left on the counter, he cried, "Ow!" The heat burned his hand. He blew on his fingers, scooped up a towel to protect his hands, and then popped the terracotta cooker into the oven.

As the clock in the living room chimed, he knew that Tennyson would be there any second. He opted to take the time to put out a couple of wine glasses and lit a candle to erase any smelly signs of his gym bag.

❖Chapter Four❖

Tennyson looked up at the one story brick house as she got the leash, hooked it to the silver loop on Mobley's collar and waited until he jumped out of the back seat of her car. She grabbed the shopping bag, and led the dog up the brick pathway. Rose bushes lined the sides. The place would be beautiful in spring. When she arrived at the door, she dropped the brass knocker twice and waited.

Par answered the door after a few seconds. He wore a dark beige suit, lavender shirt and striped tie. This night was only to help Duke find his home, but Tennyson felt an urge to run her hands under Par's coat and over his broad chest. There was a funny tingling in her fingers that she hadn't felt in a long time… a very long time. She motioned to her jeans and T-shirt and then said, "It looks as though I might be under-dressed. I thought you said a casual dinner."

He smiled, as he looked her up and then down. "You look great if anyone's asking me. Come in. Let me show you where the kitchen is. I just got home from work and haven't had time to change clothes."

"I wasn't sure what to bring, so I made a salad and brought a bottle of wine."
She handed him the shopping bag.
"The salad looks great and red's my favorite."

She waited for him to check the label or make a comment that it wasn't a good year like James always did, but he didn't. "I like to put guests to work, so if you don't mind opening the bottle, I'll be back in a few minutes."

"What's in the oven ? It smells wonderful."

"Butter chicken."

"You just got home, how did you have time to cook? It's not take-out is it?"

"No. It's not take-out." He avoided a complete answer. "You're in luck that's usually what I eat," he called as he headed down the hall and disappeared into what she guessed was the bedroom.

She found a corkscrew in the first drawer she looked in and opened the wine. She poured two glasses, stepped back and looked around the living room. It was nice and comfy. An oversized leather couch divided the dining room from the living room. He had a big screen television but other than that, the room was homey with a colorful hand-crocheted granny square blanket and pictures of his family on the fireplace mantel. Not your typical man-cave in dark colors.

Tennyson moved into the room and looked at the smiling family's photo. It was a college graduation shot. Par with his mom, dad, and a brother she assumed. His family looked proud and Par looked happy. He grinned from ear to ear. The second was a picture of Par and Boci at the beach.

"That picture was when I first got her. She was pretty scared for the first few weeks. I took time off from work and went to the ocean. I think she was terrified that I might take off and leave her, so I needed to spend some quality time with her."

Par changed into a worn gray T-shirt, faded jeans and his feet were bare. Okay, the Levi's were even sexier than the suit. *God help me.* Tennyson fought to pull her gaze back to his face.

"When I moved into my new place, Mobley didn't eat for days," she said. "Dogs get scared and depressed just like people." She bent down and picked up the chewed pillow. "Did Duke do this?"

Par took the pillow and surveyed the damage. "Probably. I've never seen Boci chew up anything. My sofa pillow was the only causality that I saw. It's not like I have a matching set. If I want a new one, I'll grab one somewhere."

"They're having a sale at *Bergman Liquidators.*" As soon as she said it, she wished she could take the words back. He'd never shop at a liquidator's store.

"Good idea," he said surprising her. "I got my couch there. If I stop by tomorrow, it's twenty-five percent off. I wonder if they have dog-proof ones. It looks as though Duke's a chewer." He grinned.

Tennyson thought of her house with James. Everything must match, he'd insisted. And there were no family photos. She assumed they weren't close like her family. James never took her to meet his family because, he said, they were always somewhere abroad on vacation

Par whistled and the three dogs ran out of the back room. "Outside you three before you destroy something else." He slid open the patio door. "I'm going to make sure the gate's latched. I'll be back in a sec."

Tennyson heard him clap his hands and then at

least two of the dogs barked. There was a knock on the door. She paused, wondering if it was out of her boundaries to answer it. She peeked through the hole and recognized Par's mother from the photo on the mantel, so she opened the door.

The woman looked a little startled. "Oh... I'm sorry. Where's Parkesh?"

"He just went out in the back with the dogs. Do you want me to get him?"

"Oh, no, do not bother. I just forgot the *Naan* that went with the dinner I brought over." She held out the foil packet. "I'm sorry to bother you two. I hope you like it."

"I'm sure I'll love it," Tennyson said. "It smells wonderful."

Just then Par came back through the door. His eyes widened with surprise. "Mom. What are you doing here?"

"She forgot the bread," Tennyson said. " The bread to go with the great dinner she made."

Even with his dark skin, Tennyson could see a blush on Par's cheeks.

"Aren't you going to introduce us?" his mother asked.

Par carried out the introductions and then led his mother to the door. Tennyson heard the woman whisper loudly, "She's very pretty."

When he shut the door, he leaned his back against the wood and closed his eyes.

"You had your mom cook dinner for us? How wonderful," she said.

He opened one eye. "I guess I'm busted. She's a

very good cook and believe me, you wouldn't want to eat anything I cooked. I was thinking of your stomach and mine. I called her earlier when I knew you were coming over."

"Why not just get take-out if you were busy?"

"I could have, but I…" his words dropped off as he cleared his throat and took the bread from her hand. He opened the oven door he slid the foil packet inside. "I wanted to impress you."

"Impress me?"

"I don't live in a fancy house or drive a fancy car. So food was a good start."

"You think I'd care about houses or cars?"

"Your last boyfriend was a lawyer, so I guessed that might be your standard of living. I have a pretty good job, but I don't spend money on things like expensive cars or houses." He threw his hands up. "I don't really know anything about you other than that you're smart, own a dog and as my mom said 'very pretty.'"

How cute is this. I like his flustered side. She tipped her head and looked up through lowered lashes. "I love your house."

"Really?"

"Really. But how about you break out that dinner your mom made, I haven't eaten since breakfast, and I'm starving."

The sun set as they finished dinner on his deck. Par felt happy he had such a large, fenced back yard with plenty of room for the dogs to run and play. He'd put up the deck umbrella and turned on the deck heater just in case Tennyson was cold. The weather was still mild for winter, but there was a nip in the air.

"That chicken tasted amazing," Tennyson said as she laid down her fork. "I ate way more than I should have. Now, I'm stuffed."

"Would you like to call my mom and tell her? It would make her day."

"You can relay the message." She turned to watch the dogs as they ran and played. "I was worried about Duke, but he looks like he's lived here all his life."

"He can stay here as long as he needs to or until we figure out what to do with him."

"I can't imagine why anyone would leave their dog behind."

He shrugged. "We can't imagine it because we'd never do it. Look what people do to their kid, it doesn't surprise me when they abuse their animals too. That's why I want to grow the foundation at my dad's company. All living things need a break sometime in their lives. Our foundation works with local farmers to use their extra crops to feed people in need. After we get the flyers made on the computer and put up around town, we can drive down there if you would like to see it."

"Sure, that sounds like fun. I don't have to be to work tomorrow until the lunch crowd."

Par was pleased she said yes. He wasn't sure how she would answer his offer. Most of the girls he's dated were high maintenance and he knew it. They would be more concerned about breaking a nail then breaking into cardboard boxes. Tennyson seemed different and someone he thought he could spend more than just an evening with. Also, when she talked about being the manager of her restaurant, she sounded as though she wanted to run the place as a team player and not a diva. What a refreshing change.

Par watched the sun reflect off her lightly tinted sunglasses and wished he could see the color of her eyes. He'd already forgotten. Were they brown? He'd studied them earlier. They were hazel with fascinating green flecks around the edges. When she smiled, it lit her face and made her nose crinkle. There was a row of faint freckles almost in a line across the bridge.

He'd never invited a girl out here in the backyard to just 'hang out.' He needed to do this more often, but only if they were as much fun as Tennyson.

Par booted up the computer in his office and created a flyer with Duke's picture in the center. Tennyson watched him work with the graphics program. His long finger flew over the keys as he quickly typed in the information. She shot a picture with his camera and he loaded it in.

When they'd printed off ten flyers, he called the dogs and locked the doors. She followed him out into the garage. The first day they'd met, she hadn't noticed what he drove. Again, Tennyson was surprised by his choice of cars. There was no low riding, red sports car parked there. Par drove a ten year old 4x4 truck with an extended cab to fit the dogs in back and a dent in the rear fender. He opened her door and then held her hand as she climbed up into the front seat.

When he got in, he laughed and swiveled in his

seat. "Hey you guys, you're fogging up the windows; stop your heavy breathing." He wiped a sleeve over the window, as he opened the garage door and headed out on the road.

They stopped on a few corners to put up the flyers near the park. Tennyson wedged her foot on the bumper, and pulled herself up to place the flyer in a more visible place.

"Careful," Par said. He entwined hands around her waist so she wouldn't fall. When she was done, his hands easily lifted her and placed her on the ground. They were warm where his fingers touched bare skin.

She turned to face him. "Thanks."

He tucked a strand of hair behind her ear. "Anytime." He brushed a thumb over her cheek. "You still want to see the warehouse?"

"Is this the best pickup line you have?"

He grinned. "No, I'm not very good at pickup lines and don't hang out in bars. I'd much rather look for girls at the dog park." When her eyes widened, he kissed the tip of her nose. He winked one of his deep chocolate brown eyes and got back in the truck.

She stood there for a second longer than she probably should have trying to clear her brain. He thought the dogs had fogged the windows? Par was fogging her brain. Every cell in her body hummed to remind her of all the things she'd been missing this past six month. Was it really time to take a chance and move on?

After he parked in the unoccupied lot, he led her into the warehouse and flipped on the lights. He brought the dogs in and shut the door. Tennyson made a full circle, surprised by the size of the place. "This place is much bigger than I imagined."

"I come and work here whenever I can. I'm hoping in a few months, my dad will let me take this over full-time, but I've already been waiting two years. He wants me to work at corporate not in a warehouse."

"Have you tried talking to him?"

"I've tried. He looks at this as a step down, where I look at it as finally getting the chance to do what I want with my life." His face darkened. Par surveyed a stack of boxes by the door. "These must have just come in." He picked up the clipboard. "It looks like they haven't logged the produce in yet."

"Can I help?"

"I didn't plan to put you to work here."

"You fed me dinner, it's the least I can do." Tennyson took the clipboard from his hands. "This looks just like the restaurant. The sheets are almost identical. I'll count up the boxes, mark them off and then you can put them wherever they go."

He still looked apprehensive.

"I wouldn't have offered if I didn't want to do it. Come on and get to work." Opening the first bushel boxes, Tennyson counted the heads of cabbage. As she pulled the boxes to the side, Par lifted them and then placed them on the steel shelving in the back.

She pulled a hair tie from her pocket, wound her hair up in a ponytail and moved to the next box. She lifted a pen and checked off the contents.

As Par came back for the next box, he frowned, as he wiped his forehead, "Your shirt's all dirty."

Tennyson looked down. There was a big black smudge across her mid-section. "Oh no," she said and then shrugged. "That's what I get for wearing white. Dark colors are more my color so they don't show dirt. Thank goodness they let us stop wearing white shirts at work, I was always spilled things on myself."

He picked up the box from the floor and swung it onto his shoulders. He whistled and the dogs ran out from behind a set of shelves to follow him down the row. She watched him saunter away. The suit was nice, but that backside in a nice pair of jeans? Again, *oh…my*.

Not watching where she was going. Tennyson stumbled back and knocked into the next set of boxes. The stack tilted. She grabbed for it and caught most of them, but a wooden lettuce box tilted and then hit her in the back of the ankle. "Ow!" she cried.

Par ran towards her and straightened the stack. She hopped on one foot looking for a place to sit. He led her to an empty crate.

"Are you okay?" Concern etched his face.

"I'm just a klutz. Ow!" She rubbed the back of her ankle.

He knelt before her. "Let me see your foot." He lifted her leg out straight and turned her ankle. "You took some skin off. Let me run and get an ice pack from the freezer and a washcloth."

He came back in a few minutes with the ice. He helped her take off her shoe and placed the pack on the back of her leg. "If you can get back to the truck, I better get you home before I do any more damage."

Tennyson was angry with herself that she ruined the fun evening. This was why she shouldn't date. Par put Boci and Duke in the house and then Mobley in her backseat, then came around and helped her out of the truck.

"Keep ice on that the rest of the night. I hope it doesn't swell." He leaned into the cab of his truck and pulled out a pad of paper. "This is my work number. If you need to go to the doctor or need me for anything, please don't hesitate to call."

Was she ready for the next step? "I'm a little old for kissing boo-boo's but I'll take a kiss on the lips instead."

"I broke you." He watched her with intense dark eyes. "I bet you think this was the worst date ever."

"You didn't break me; I *bruised* myself by being klutzy." She wiggled her foot. "See."

He looked down at her foot and then back up before he stepped closer. "So I only broke you a little bit?"

"Just a little…" her words trailed as she swallowed deeply. He smelled like pine trees and fresh air.

"I'm happy this wasn't your worst date ever, because I had a great time." He lifted her chin with the tips of his finger. Slowly he lowered his head until she thought she would die of anticipation. He clamped his hands to her waist and gazed into her eyes. "You're so beautiful…" There was depth and sincerity in the tone of his voice. She felt special. Desired. He dropped his head and kissed her.

Gentle at first and then deep. She couldn't breathe. He'd sucked all the air from her lungs, but there was no way she wanted him to stop. As she brushed his firm lips to hers, she relished the feel of her blood simmering in her veins. Par slid his fingers through her long hair to cradle and position her head to kiss her even more thoroughly.

His lips pulled away from hers and he stepped back. She reached for the roof of the car to steady herself. *Oh. My. God. Could this man kiss.*

"Not bad for a first date," he whispered and then kissed her gently again.

Okay. So it *was* a date. After that kiss it turned into an 'official date' and she had no regrets at all.

❖Chapter Five❖

Par called Tennyson daily over the last few weeks. Tennyson checked on Duke on a regular basis. Duke's owners didn't step up and Par didn't get any calls on the flyers. Since they abandoned Duke, Par doubted that they would. But that was okay, the extra dog grew on him. It gave Boci companionship during the day when he was away.

Last night, Tennyson stayed for a glass of wine, but not nearly long enough for Par's liking. Christmas was just around the corner, and all he wanted for Christmas was to spend more time with her. At work, Par filled his afternoons trying to think of topics of conversation he could engage her in to make her stay longer. It was more difficult each time she walked out the door because he wanted more. He wanted her. Tennyson was becoming as much a part of his life as Duke.

Every time he'd tried to ask her out on a *real* date, not a 'dog date', as she called them, she hesitated and made an excuse. He didn't think it was because she didn't like him—or he hoped that was the case. She'd been burned and was wary of striking up another relationship. She'd told him more about her break up. *Brutal.* James hooked up with her high-school friend and then packed her stuff in reusable grocery bags and kicked her to the curb? Literally. The man was cold, uptight, and uncaring.

Par'd gotten those vibes from James whenever they were in the same room and it made Par wonder what she'd even seen in the man. In office meetings with

James, the jerk bragged about this car and that vacation. No one in the office cared, but James talked on and on about his new purchases and what he called his *trophy fiancé*. Did he love this poor girl or was he only marrying her because she was blonde and beautiful? Tennyson was one of the most beautiful women Par'd ever met, inside and out. James must be crazy to have let her go.

Par had a few hours that night, so if she wouldn't come to him, he'd try to see her at *The Neighborhood Grill*. He didn't want to come across as desperate or worse yet a stalker. He just wanted to see her but not push boundaries.

Music boiled out of the bar decorated in a British pub feel. Stained glass panels hung over the bar and brass beer pulls shone in the light. A few couples played pool on the rustic wood tables. While he waited to be seated, he took note of the section Tennyson worked.

When he spotted her, he said to the server, "I think I'll eat in the bar tonight." She waved him through and gave him the once over. Funny, a month ago he would have winked back and maybe asked the woman for her number. Now… well, everyone paled in comparison to Tennyson. He slid into a booth and waited until she turned and spotted him.

"Hey, I didn't expect to see you tonight." Her smile was genuine.

"I'm justifying my actions of stopping by for two reasons. One, I love the food here. Two, I figured if I stopped to eat dinner, then I could swing by the house, pick up the dogs and still have a few hours to work at the food bank and not have to cook."

"Sounds like a plan. The Copper River salmon is the special tonight. You told me that it's your favorite. I can have the cooks hold you a piece if you're interested."

"You remembered. Sounds like the perfect meal, but I'll take a glass of red first. Are you off work soon? Will you have dinner with me?"

"I'm off in about ten minutes." She hesitated and bit her lip. "Things are good between us, Par, but I just don't want to rush things. I did that the last time and it didn't work out well."

He didn't want to push, but as he looked into her beautiful brown eyes he knew that he couldn't let it stand without asking. "Do I have a chance? Because I'm really beginning to like you. Is it the right time? The right place? Are you waiting for a different man? What are you looking for?"

She shrugged. "I guess, what every girl wants. To be swept off her feet with a little song and dance. But, this time, it has to be more than just for show. I just don't know if I'm ready." She looked around. "I'll get your wine and then ask the owner if I can get off a little early. Let me ask the cooks if they can prepare two salmon dinners. If he'll let me off, I'll think about having dinner with you."

"You'll have dinner with me for a little song and dance."

She grinned. "Yeah, but you better make it good." And then she disappeared into the kitchen.

Par looked across the bar and got an idea. He took a deep breath to gather his nerves and headed out across the dance floor. Lucky him, it was karaoke night.

The DJ looked up and slid his earphones on top of his head as Par approached.

"Do you happen to have; *Dog Days are Over* by Florence and the Machine?"

"Sure. You going solo, or you got someone who's singing with you?"

"This one will have to be solo. Can you start it when I tell you?" He waited until he saw Tennyson appear at the bar and order his wine. "Okay." He grabbed the mic. The music started and Par began to sing.

Tennyson walked to his table, set the glass down, and looked around. When she saw him on the stage, her eyes widened.

She said she wanted song and dance, and she'd get it. He fought the urge to look at the lyrics on the monitor, but convinced himself he knew the song by heart. Instead, Par looked at Tennyson and poured his heart out.

She moved toward the stage. She wasn't smiling at first, but then broke into a huge grin. Par tried not to sigh in relief between bars of the song. When he finished, she clapped enthusiastically along with the rest of the bar.

He thanked the DJ and then stepped off the stage.

"You never told me that you could sing!" she exclaimed. "I always pegged you for more of the strait-laced exec type; never a goof who sings karaoke."

"There's a lot you don't know about me." He took her hand and kissed the back of her knuckles. "I was in a garage band in college. I played bass and never sang more than back-up, but we were good enough for a few free beers. We played cover songs and this was one of the songs that we sang."

She raised an eyebrow. "The song you chose, *Dog Days are Over*, were you trying to tell me something about my life… the four-legged kind excluded?"

"I knew you'd pick up the double entendre. You wanted a guy who can sing and dance you off your feet. Here I am."

"I didn't mean literally."

"You know how much guts it took to get up there and sing? I can't do it again. I haven't consumed nearly enough liquid courage."

"It was a great rendition." She looked up through lowered lashes and squeezed his hand. His heart did a funny little skip, the way it always did when Tennyson was around.

❖Chapter Six❖

After she'd worked a full eight-hour shift and then stayed out longer than she'd planned for dinner with Par, she was exhausted. Tennyson ran a quick comb through her hair, brushed her teeth and fell asleep as soon as her head hit the pillow.

She woke up to a ruckus outside her bedroom door. She rolled over to look at the digital glowing clock.

Two o'clock

She groaned and rubbed sleep from her eyes as Shelly opened her door. The light from the hall made her blink.

"Mobley ran past me, I tried to stop him but he was too fast," Shelly said with a little hiccup. Shelly'd gone out with some girlfriends and she'd been drinking.

"You go to bed. I'll get him." Tennyson rolled over, fighting not to fall back asleep. Finally she got up, pulled on her robe and went to the back door. Mobley was at the bottom of the stairs. "Come on, boy." She patted her leg for him to follow.

Mobley tried to stand but then whined and sat back down. She clapped again, but still he didn't come up the stairs. Barefoot, she descended the stairs. That was when she saw the blood on his hind leg and noticed it stuck out at a strange angle.

Tennyson cried out and flew down the last few steps. Mobley looked up at her with big brown eyes and whimpered. Quickly, she checked the rest of him. The blood seemed come from his hip. Grabbing his collar, she hooked him to the railing so he wouldn't try to move again.

She ran back into the house, and searched for Shelly who already lay on top of her bed. Tennyson tried to wake her up, but Shelly grumbled and rolled over onto her stomach. She'd had too much to drink and shouldn't drive. Tennyson remembered her mom and dad were gone on vacation, so there was no one. She wasn't in any condition to drive either— she was a mass of anxious tension— but she would if she needed to.

Then she remembered there was someone. With shaking hands, Tennyson rummaged through her purse until she found the card she was looking for and punched in the number. She waited until a sleepy voice answered, "Hello?"

"Par?" Her voice broke with emotion. "Mobley got outside... I think he's been hit by a car."

"Oh my, God. Is he still alive?"

"Yes... he's alive... but... there's a lot of blood. What should I do?"

"I'll be right there."

Tennyson dropped her phone into her pocket and ran back out to Mobley. He was breathing heavy, but wagged his tail when he saw her. That made her cry harder. Unconditional love, even when he was in pain.

Par's truck pulled up in less than five minutes. He jumped out and jogged toward them. "How's he doing?" Worry was evident on his face.

"I don't know." She wiped her eyes with the back

of her hand. "He was only outside a few minutes. If I'd gotten up when Shelly told me to, this wouldn't have happened."

"Don't blame yourself. It was an accident." Par put an arm around her and gave her a hug. He knelt and took a quick survey of Mobley. "It's his hind leg. We'd better go."

"It's two o'clock in the morning. What place will be open?"

"There's a twenty-four hour vet hospital about fifteen minutes away." He wrapped the blanket around Mobley that she'd brought out. "Can you open the side door of my truck?" Gently he lifted the dog and placed him on the back seat. When he turned, Par looked down at her bare legs underneath her pajama shorts. "Why don't you run in and put on some jeans? You'll freeze out here. I'll call ahead and tell them what we know about the injury so they will be prepared."

She nodded and dashed back up the stairs. After she threw on a sweatshirt and pants, she scribbled a note to Shelly to tell her what happened. It wasn't Shelly's fault; Mobley always tried to run out. He needed to be somewhere with a fenced yard and not in an apartment next to a busy road.

Tennyson opened the back door and slid in next to Mobley. He put his head in her lap and looked up at her with his big brown eyes.

Par swiveled and put a hand on her knee.

"He's my responsibility. He's all I have," she said trying not to cry again.

"Not all, but I know how important he is. He's a great dog. He'll be okay." He turned the truck around and headed back out on the road.

When they arrived at the vet's office, the staff waited outside with a dog size gurney. They took Mobley back into the emergency room and left Par and Tennyson in the waiting area. After watching her pace for a few minutes, he took her hand. "Let's sit down. They'll be out as soon as there's any news."

He put an arm around her shoulders and pulled her under his arm. Par buried his head in her hair and whispered, "Don't cry. He'll be okay. They'll take care of him."

About an hour later, the vet came out and pulled off his blue mask. "Well there's good news and bad news. There are no internal injuries, but we're going to have to do surgery to wire Mobley's hip back into place. The injury was severe enough that the ball joint won't pop back in. His hip will need more than that, so we'll do the surgery in the morning."

"Thank you, Doctor," Tennyson said, her voice small.

Par stood behind Tennyson while she filled out the paperwork. After Par convinced her to let him take her home and not sleep in the waiting room, before they left, she told Mobley one more time that she would be back tomorrow. They rode in silence until they reached her apartment.

Her eyes were red from crying. He wished he could take away the pain.

"Thanks for being there tonight. I didn't know who else to call."

"To rebut what you said earlier, I hope that you know you have someone in your life other than Mobley. You can call me anytime, day or night and I'll be here for you."

"Yes… I'm beginning to believe that." Tennyson watched him for a long moment. "It's taking time but the walls are coming down. Thanks for all you've done."

He cupped her cheek. "I'll pick you up in the morning. You can see Mobley before and then after he gets out of surgery."

"You don't have to do that."

"What if I want to?"

She sniffed. "You're a nice guy, do you know that?"

"I'll be here by nine. The doctor said the surgery is at ten, so we can pick up coffee on the way and it will give you time to kiss his nose and get a sloppy dog kiss."

Par played with Boci and Duke a few minutes and then went in to work early. He'd slept little during the night. It was decision-making time and that was never easy, but he wouldn't let any more of his life slip by.

Even though it was only a little past seven, Par knew his dad would already be at work. He rapped his knuckles on his office door.

As he finished his conversation, his father waved him in. After he'd set the phone back on the desk he said, "Parkash, you are never here this early."

"Yeah, I am Dad… every morning. On most days I'm here by six."

"Well that's good. Hard work will bring you happiness."

Par dropped into a chair and leaned forward. "I need some time off."

"Time off?" his father's voice rose up on the last word. "How much *time off?*"

"I'm not sure. A few weeks?" He pulled in a breath. "When I come back, I want you to find a replacement for me so I can work at the foundation and food bank full-time."

His father waved his hand. "Don't be silly. That is not the job for you."

"It *is* the job for me. That is what I want."

"No, here is where you will work."

"Then, I'm handing in my resignation. You promised me if I put in the hours and did everything you asked, that I could be put in charge of the foundation and the food bank. If you're rescinding that offer, then I'll have to leave."

His father watched him through narrowed eyes. "You can have the time off, if that is what you want."

Par shook his head. "Thanks, I'll take it, but the rest still stands. Father, I owe everything to you, you're a great man. You've sacrificed so much for your family and worked hard in your life at jobs I can never imagine doing. For that I admire you. But, I need to create my own destiny with what I feel passionate about."

"Is this about the woman your mother told me that you are seeing?"

"No..." then he paused. "Yes. But this decision isn't hers, its mine. Her dog was accidently hit last night and I want to be there for her. I don't know if she can take time off, but I can."

"This is over a dog?"

"This is over caring for something and someone. You love mother and us boys. I want to have the time in my life to find that kind of relationship. Working twelve to fifteen hour days makes it difficult to do little more. I don't want the money, but I want the love and the life. Can you understand that?"

His father paused before he nodded. "Yes, Parkash. I want that for you too. I know how hard you work, and as you know I'm a man of my word. You take the time you need off and then when you get back we will move you into the acting head of the foundation."

Par leapt up and hugged his dad. "Thanks!"

❖Chapter Seven❖

"Mobley's back haunch is healing better than expected," Doctor Carlson said.

"I'm so happy that I can take him home today." Tennyson scratched him under the collar. "He looks a bit like Frankenstein's dog being shaved and with all the stitches on his hip, but I'm so happy he's alive."

"Just watch him," the doctor cautioned, "and make sure he doesn't go up and down any stairs."

"I live in a small apartment that has a dozen stairs," Tennyson said.

The doctor looked down at Mobley and then shook his head. "That won't work. He needs to be on one level for at least two weeks. If the surgery area is damaged, then he might have to go in for another operation and neither of us wants that."

"He can stay at my house," Par offered. "I'll keep him in the laundry room for a few days and follow him out with the other two dogs to make sure he takes it easy."

"That should work," the doctor said. "Well, I wish Mobley all the best. He's been a favorite patient of mine."

When the girl at the front desk slid the white paper bill over the desk, Tennyson took her credit card out of her leather wallet and frowned.

"Is everything okay?" Par asked, concern on his face.

"It's a lot more than I thought it would be," she whispered.

After a minute the girl came back and held the credit card between two fingers. "I'm sorry, the card was declined."

Tennyson's mind spun trying to think of an option. "I can borrow some money when my parents are back from Hawaii. They don't have a phone right now, but they'll be back by Friday."

"I'm sorry," the girl said apologetically. "We need payment before we can release your pet."

Par took out a card and handed it to the girl. "Here, use mine."

"I can't let you do this," Tennyson said reaching for his wrist.

"Look…" He took her arm and led her to the other side of the waiting room and out of ear shot of the receptionist. "I care about Mobley and I care about you. This money doesn't come with a catch or any promises you aren't ready for. We need to resolve this and get Mobley home. I have the money on my card and you can pay me back if that's what you want."

"It will take me five years to pay back that much."

"It will take the same amount of time if you put it on a charge card, and I won't charge you interest. I'll tell you what. I need a reliable produce checker at the food bank. The gal we're paying now is worthless. If you can work there, say four hours a week, you can pay me back as you put in the hours. I really could use the help. But right now, Mobley wants to get out of here. What do you say?"

"I don't know what to say."

There was a moment of hurt in the depth of his eyes. "Maybe someday… you will."

Christmas Eve arrived cold and damp. The temperature dropped and the dark gray clouds threatened snow. Tennyson thought if she was snowed in for a few days with Par… it could definitely be worse. Mobley's hip was healing well and he was back to playing and running with the other two dogs.

Tennyson sat cross-legged on the couch next to Par. "It doesn't look as though Duke's owners will ever come back. What should we do?"

"I could never give him up now or take him to the Humane Society or a shelter. I've become way too attached. One more is no trouble."

"What about two more? I think Mobley has set up a permanent dwelling here too."

"That's okay." He smiled. "They keep each other occupied, but the squirrels are in big trouble with three hoodlums out in the yard now. Mobley's loving it here."

"Bringing Mobley here to heal was a great idea. He fits in like he's been here his whole life." Tennyson reached into her purse and pulled out a small bag. "I spotted this today in a shop window downtown. It's a thank you for all you've done."

"*Ganesha*," Par said, as he opened the bag and slid out the tiny half-man half-elephant ornaments. "Do you know that this is the Hindu god known for the lord of beginnings and the remover of obstacles?"

"I read about Ganesha in a book the other day. I thought I'd pick up two. One for each of us. I think we can use a little help from the gods."

"Are you ready for a new beginning, Tennyson? I know I am. I removed one of my life's obstacles the other day when I told my dad that I'd quit if he didn't hold true to his word."

"Are you happy you talked to him?"

"Yes, but it was difficult. I've never really questioned his authority before. I'm sure it was a surprise to him too. I know that once I get into my new position and he has my replacement trained he'll see it's for the best." Par rose from the couch and hung the ornament on the tree. "Here, hang yours too.'

Tennyson took the ornament and placed it on a branch next to his.

"Dad can't be that mad," Par said. "He invited us both to dinner tomorrow. Your parents are still gone, right? Do you have any other plans?"

When he turned to face her, Tennyson laid a hand on his chest. "Will it be okay? You told me your family wanted you to find 'a nice Indian girl.' I'm Italian and just because the countries start with the same letter, I don't think it counts."

He scooted closer. "Mom said she liked you, especially after you complimented her on her Naan. She's looking forward to showing you how to bake it."

"Wait, you celebrate a Christmas? You're Hindu."

"Sure. Where do you think I got all those ornaments? My family believes in melding as many beliefs as possible. They believe in family, gathering and food.

It's a great time of the year for all of that, don't you think?"

"It is. That and much more." She pulled him in for a kiss. Long and sweet. When she stepped back, she said, "I got something else for you. It's nothing big; I got it at Bergman's." She went to the front door and brought back a large wrapped package.

He yanked off the paper. "A karaoke machine, for home. You're kidding me! This is great." He laughed and tugged it out of the box.

She pointed to the lettering. "I got it because it says right on the front, '*All the Old Favorites including Hound Dog*,' so I thought that was pretty perfect. It's also a stereo and MP3 player if you just want to listen to music."

"I can't wait to use it." He leaned over and pulled out a rectangular gold-wrapped box. "Here's something for you."

"You've given me enough helping out with Mobley's vet bill. I don't need presents."

"It's something I think you'll want."

She laid a hand on his. "I have everything I want."

"Not everything… open it, will ya? I've been dying to give this to you for a week."

She slid off the shiny gold paper, opened the cardboard and stared inside. Her heart filled until she thought it would burst. Tennyson looked up at Par. "It's my grandmother's jewelry box. How did you…"

"I was in James's office for a business meeting. I remembered you said it was the only thing you wished you'd been able to get back from the relationship but he'd kept it. Since you didn't mention it again, I assumed he still had it. That night you described it. I recognized it on his desk. He had Christmas candy in it. When I complimented him on it, he said I could have it. That was when I took it, thanked him, and then told him that we were seeing each other. I also told him that when he left you it was the best thing that ever happened to me."

"You really said that?"

"You bet I did. You should have seen his face drop. What did you call him… asshat? I bet the only thing he thought was that I would have my father fire his firm. I would if it was up to me, but it's not my division and now that I'm at the foundation, I won't ever have to see him."

She ran her hand over the cut crystal. "You don't know how much this box means to me. My grandmother gave it to me right before she died. I never thought I'd see it again. You got it back for me."

"I knew it was special."

"And I got you a karaoke machine."

"I love karaoke."

Tennyson set the box on the table and then moved into his arms. "Speaking of that…"

"Karaoke."

"No… love. I swore off men *and* love, but now that I look back, I realize I was never in love with James. I thought I was, but I was in love with the idea, not the man."

"What about me?" Par looked into her eyes.

"You said maybe someday I'd know what to say. Tonight and for the last few weeks I've known what to say but wanted to be sure. I love you, Par. I know it's crazy and quick… and Christmas, but I love you."

He put a thumb under her chin and tipped it up. "I've known it for a long time and I hoped that you were ready too. I know I am. You made me realize what's important in life. Money's nice to have to pay for the important things but it doesn't bring happiness. You and Mobley are what do that."

"What about Duke and Boci?"

"Yeah, them too."

Tennyson was so happy she could burst. She closed her eyes, as she felt the warmth of his body engulf her and pull her close. Then he kissed her. Slow at first and then with a white-hot intensity that's she'd never remembered from any kiss. His mouth was warm against her and then he broke away only to nibble down her neck.

His hands came back to her face, cupping her cheeks in his palms.

Par covered his mouth with hers and she savored the taste and warmth of him. This is what had always been missing with James. Her mind swam and her body pulsed with wonderful sensations. Tennyson wanted this moment to go on for the rest of her life, and if she had any say, it would.

As if he could read her mind, Par pulled her tight against him and kissed her until she felt light-headed.

When he finally stepped back, he plugged in the karaoke machine, scanned the data and hit play.

"It's not very Christmassy, but oh well." *Hound Dog* blasted over the speakers. Par grabbed her hand, spun her around in the middle of the living room and began to sing. He twisted his leg and foot into the carpet, and added moves Elvis might have envied.

"What are you doing? You're crazy!" she exclaimed as he spun her around again.

"You said you wanted a man with song and dance, so I'm going to sing for you and dance with you, and then if it's okay, I want to make love to you all night long."

"I think that sounds like the best Christmas present ever."

Wondering if they were missing out on something, the three dogs ran out from the back barking wildly. Duke jumped up and knocked Par back onto the couch. He laughed as he tried to push him to the side. "Get off me you big tugboat."

Tennyson piled on him along with the other two dogs.

"This is complete mayhem!" he attempted to yell over the barking.

"Yes! Isn't it perfect? I love you. Merry Christmas!" she shouted and threw her arms wide. She reached back, grabbed a Santa hat and then drew it over his black hair. "Come here, Mr. Hindu Claus." She kissed him again along with the sloppy dog kisses he got from all directions. She laughed until her sides hurt.

This time, Tennyson knew she'd made the right decision. This time she'd let her heart lead. She got the dog—actually three dogs—and the best guy in the world.

A NOTE FROM THE AUTHOR

Every dog needs a loving home. Duke is an actual shelter
dog. He's my big, silly, eight-year-old lab I adopted as a
shelter dog last year. He was eight when I adopted him...
it would have been tough for him to find a new home,
but I took the chance with an older dog. Now he's part of
our family.
If you are thinking of bringing a rescue/shelter dog into
your life here are some links:
http://www.aspca.org/pet-care/virtual-pet-
behaviorist/dog-behavior/adopting-shelter-dog
My local dog rescues:
http://www.rescueeverydog.org/
http://www.pasadosafehaven.org/
http://olddoghaven.org/

Halo's Wish
Sharon Kleve

❖Chapter One❖

Autumn in Seattle

Halo Carlyle worked for Green Hornet Investigations as a pet detective; retrieving lost and stolen animals. Her current assignment, filling in as a temporary receptionist involved searching for evidence that would implicate Pemsky Security in the recent thefts and ransoming of prize dogs from the Western Washington Dog Shows (WWDS).

The president of the WWDS strongly suspected Pemsky's company. Shortly before the thefts occurred, Pemsky's Security fees increased, but not their level of service. As a result, the WWDS Board terminated their five-year contract. He hadn't taken the news well and subsequently, dogs went missing.

Corny Myers, Halo's boss at Green Hornet Investigations, heard Pemsky's regular receptionist would be on vacation. She sent Halo over to his office and instructed her to, *show a little leg and act eager to please.* He'd hired Halo on the spot and insisted paying her under the table. She'd agreed, of course.

Pemsky ran his business old-school and kept paper copies of all his records in file cabinets, which should've made her search easier. So far Halo's efforts to snoop were hindered because he'd arrive before her and leave after she did.

At the end of the day, Halo gathered her purse to leave and peeked around Pemsky's office door. She'd watched him hide the master key to all his cabinets under his keyboard drawer. What luck! She should only need an hour alone in his office to hunt through the records and be able to confirm one way or another Pemsky's involvement in the thefts. She'd have to be patient and wait for the right opportunity.

The next morning, Halo placed a call through to Pemsky's office, which went straight to his voicemail, when the front office door opened. Halo smiled and looked up into dreamy, gold-flecked green eyes, short sandy brown hair, a slight cleft chin, and full lips set in a hard line. Even with his stern look, her hormones jumped into overdrive.

Mr. Dreamy cleared his throat. She must've been staring. In her most professional voice she greeted him, "Good morning. How may I help you?"

He removed a piece of paper from his shirt pocket and unfolded the sheet.

"I was parked in front of the Beacon Hill Ale House and my driver's side mirror was sideswiped by one of Pemsky's Security SUVs Friday night."

Halo loved the Beacon Hill Ale House. Every Saturday night, the Ale House allowed local bands to jam together. That's where she'd met her last loser boyfriend. She'd had a lot of loser boyfriends. She'd put dating on the back-burner, but wouldn't mind jumping back into the dating game for this dreamboat.

He handed her the slip of paper.

"I wasn't able to get a look at the driver, but I got the license plate number of the vehicle that hit my car and *drove away.*"

"I'm very sorry about your car. I'm sure Mr. Pemsky will be happy to cover the damage." Halo checked the company log and Pemsky's name popped up as the driver. She gulped.

Mr. Dreamy spoke again.

"I've called several times and left messages. He hasn't returned any of my calls."

Typical behavior for Pemsky, plus he had a stack of past due notices piled up on his desk.

"Again, I'm very sorry. I'm only working here temporarily, until the regular receptionist gets back from vacation." Halo felt bad for him. If someone bashed her car, she wouldn't be calm, like he seemed to be. "What is your name? I'll check to see if Mr. Pemsky is available to see you now."

"Richard McFarland."

"Mr. McFarland, please have a seat. Can I get you something to drink while you wait?"

"No. I'm fine. Thank you."

His voice softened but he stood in front of her desk with his legs parted, arms crossed over his broad chest, while she picked up the phone to notify Mr. Pemsky. His phone rang several times, but he never answered. If he'd stepped out to use the restroom she would've seen him pass by her desk. Maybe he passed out from too many carbs and caffeine. He drank gallons of cheap black coffee, and his lunches consisted of a double cheeseburger and supersized fries.

After he'd consumed his greasy lunch, he'd shove a fat cigar in his mouth and slide the brown slug from side to side. She'd never actually seen him light the nasty thing up, though. She warned him about the amount of caffeine, and cholesterol he consumed, but he rudely told her to mind her own business.

What could you expect from a possible dog thief?

"Excuse me. I'll just be a moment." Halo stood, rubbed the creases out of the front of her new skirt, and tried to look like she'd mastered high-heels.

Halo stood outside Pemsky's door, but didn't hear a peep, grunt, or snort. Normal sounds that emanated from his office. She knocked twice like he'd instructed her to before entering. His chair twisted from side-to-side, like he'd just gotten up. She bent down and checked the floor in case he'd toppled out of his chair from an overdose of sludge.

Pemsky's sweat-coated body sat propped up against the back wall. He panted in short, quick breaths.

Crap!

She knelt beside him and took his clammy hand in hers. He squeezed back hard.

"Girly, help me. I'm going to die," he wheezed.

"Okay… I need to call for help. I can't reach the phone unless you let go of my hand." He didn't release her, only squeezed harder.

Halo heard the slight creak of his door. She stretched her neck to look over the top of Pemsky's desk. Mr. McFarland followed her in. After taking in the situation, he removed his jacket and rolled up his sleeves.

100

He pushed Pemsky's leather chair out of the way and knelt beside her.

"What's going on here?" he asked.

"I don't know. I found him like this. I'm really worried. Can you call for the paramedics for me?" Halo said in a rush. Pemsky's face alternated between red and pasty white. He moaned and squeezed her hand again. The bones in her fingers ground together.

"I'm dying, that's what's going on. My chest is killing me. Call for help already," Pemsky choked out.

"Try and stay calm, Mr. Pemsky. We'll get you help," she reassured him.

Mr. McFarland stood up, took out his cell phone from his pant pocket, and dialed 9-1-1, while Halo pried each of her fingers out of Pemsky's damp hand. Once she'd finished, she stroked his arm to soothe him. He might be a liar, thief, and definitely a jerk, but he must have some redeeming qualities, she hadn't been introduced to yet.

He talked in a quiet voice to the 9-1-1 operator, but she heard him say, "We have a man, in his mid-fifties, in need of medical attention. He's conscience and able to speak. There's a possibility he's having a heart attack."

The operator must've asked their location, because he looked around and picked up a piece of stationary and rattled off the address.

"Tell them the center of my chest is burning and my arms hurt. I'm dizzy, nauseated, and I threw up my lunch. I'm having a freaking heart attack. Send an ambulance," Pemsky pleaded.

Mr. McFarland looked concerned and repeated what Pemsky said to the operator. Pemsky grabbed his chest again and closed his eyes. Halo moved past worried, and moved straight into panic mode.

Please don't die, please don't die…

"Medical aid is on the way, try and stay calm. You're going to be fine," Mr. McFarland said in a reassuring voice.

Pemsky fidgeted with the hem of his shirt, while they waited for the paramedics to arrive. Halo took ahold of his other hand and rubbed her thumb over the top, more for her benefit than his. She wanted to feel the blood flow through his veins. After what seemed like an eternity, the paramedics bustled in the door with a butt load of equipment. After an initial evaluation, they loaded him onto a gurney. Pemsky had enough strength left for a nasty remark as they wheeled him out his office door.

"Make sure to lock up when you leave, and if you leave early, I'm not paying you for a full day," Pemsky said with a huff.

"I hope he's going to be okay," she whispered.

"Your boss doesn't seem like a very nice guy."

"He's acting like a jerk now because he's scared. He has a really nice wife and three young boys. See that picture on his desk? That's them. He calls them all the time."

"Nice picture. I'm sure he'll be fine." He extended his hand. "Call me Rich. What's your name?"

"Halo." His hand felt cool and dry to the touch, but a little bit rough. That roughness would feel good on smooth skin, like the underside of her breast.

Stop, cease, and desist that train of thought. You are focusing on your career, not a nice, sexy, kind, great-looking guy. Forget about Rich before you do something stupid, like give the calluses a test drive on your inner thigh.

He followed her back to the reception area and stood in front of her. Halo backed up a step to put a little distance between them, caught her heel on the carpet and stumbled. He steadied her by grasping her shoulders and backed her up against the desk. He released her shoulders, brushed a strand of hair out of her face, and tucked it behind her ear.

Don't look into his eyes…Look away.

"Are you okay?" he asked with humor in his voice.

"Yes, I'm okay. I'm just new to this walking thing." He backed up, but not before he tucked another strand of curly hair behind her ear.

Halo's stomach did a flip-flop from the emotions he'd stirred up.

"Is Halo your given name?"

He didn't laugh at her name, like most people, but seemed genuinely interested. "My mother swore I emerged into this world with a shining halo above my head. My dad said the effect seemed to come from sunlight shining through the delivery room blinds. Either way, they named me Halo Ann Carlyle."

"Halo… the name fits you. You know, you handled a very stressful situation amazingly well. I admire that. Would you like to go to lunch?"

He appeared to be educated and well-dressed— Not her usual type.

"I can't. I need to notify Mr. Pemsky's wife that he's on the way to the hospital. And I have a lot of work to do before I can leave for the day."

"You sure are a loyal temporary employee. Especially after the way your boss treated you. You most likely saved his life."

"For his family's sake, I really hope he gets better. I told him he needs to eat right and exercise, but he laughed at me."

"Halo, you're a really nice person. Pemsky doesn't deserve your dedication," Rich said, while he shook his head.

"Maybe not." She thought for a moment and made a moral decision. "I guess it couldn't hurt to tell you that the driver of the SUV was Pemsky."

"Really… I was willing to let the hit-and-run go if Pemsky would take care of the repair, but now I'll let my insurance company handle the claim."

He hadn't backed up very far and she smelled something scrumptious. Rich smelled like a warm sea breeze, salty and fresh. She must've been staring again because he winked at her.

"Do you have a boyfriend?"

"No, I'm on a hiatus from dating. I'm focusing on my career." His smile didn't falter.

"What time do you get off work?" he asked, and smiled brighter.

"I'm usually off by five o'clock, but I'll have to work later tonight. I have a lot of filing to catch up on."

"You said the position here was temporary. Do you have another job waiting for you?"

"Yes, I do. I appreciate your help today, but I really should get back to work." Halo headed toward the door, in hopes that he'd follow her.

"Rich," he said, as he rested his hip against her desk.

"What?" She turned and realized he hadn't moved. What a stubborn sucker. She'd looked in the mirror this morning and like every day she saw the same thing: an oval face, with a few freckles scattered around her fair completion, and unruly, brown curly hair. Today her faux tortoise-shell clips lost their battle to hold her curls in place. Ringlets sprouted like corkscrews in every direction. Did Rich see more?

He pushed himself away from her desk and headed in her direction, his eyes half closed, his lips parted, she knew sexual desire when she saw it. Luckily his cell rang. Talk about saved by the bell.

"Hello? I'm about fifteen minutes away. I'll be right there. Try and keep her calm. Yeah, she likes her belly stroked. Okay, I'm on my way."

Now, *that* intrigued her.

"Everything okay?" Halo asked.

"Yes, but I've got to go. Cleo's giving birth. I'll be back, though. Why don't you give me your number?"

"By your call it sounds as though you have your hands full. Maybe you should stick to one female at a time?" She hated cheaters, especially blatant ones.

"Huh?" He looked perplexed for a moment, and then smiled. "Oh, I'm a veterinarian at McFarland Veterinary. My clinic is on Beacon Hill and Cleo is a sweet, scared dog that wandered into my parking lot a couple weeks ago. She didn't have a microchip and nobody's claimed her. She's about ready to give birth and I want to be there for her."

"Sorry, I thought you were talking about your wife."

Me and my big mouth.

"No, I'm not married or in a relationship—yet."

Halo ignored the 'yet' comment.

"What kind of dog is she?" Hey, she loved animals too.

"Cleo's a small, short-haired, mixed breed. She's at my place. My neighbor's been keeping an eye on her while I'm at work. That's who called. I have a couple acres out in Enumclaw, which I share with a menagerie of animals I can't find homes for. I can't understand why people have pets and then abuse or neglect them."

"I feel the same way. You'd better hurry. Cleo needs you."

He did the most unexpected thing; he lifted her hand and brushed his lips across the top. When she pulled her hand back, he took her face in his hands and brushed those same lips over hers. He trailed those lips down the side of her neck, and then stepped back.

"I'll be seeing you, sweet Halo," he said before he left.

Man, he had smoking hot lips. Her spine shot sparklers to her brain.

❖Chapter Two❖

The minute Rich left, Halo rushed into Pemsky's office and pushed and pulled on all of his file drawers. She'd hoped he'd forgotten to lock them, but no such luck. She hadn't considered how she'd get into his keyboard tray to get his key. Her heel caught on a loose carpet thread and twisted her ankle and bumped the desk with her hip. "Darn, darn. That hurt!"

When she hit the desk, Pemsky's keyboard tray popped open an inch. Bingo! Using the key, she carefully searched through all of Pemsky's files, trying not to disturb anything.

Halo scoured through records labeled; business meals, business travel, and business taxes. And then, under business equipment, she hit paydirt—records of all the money transfers from the stolen blue ribbon dogs to his personal bank account at Seattle Mutual Bank. In another folder, labeled miscellaneous business expenses, were payment transfers to a local bank account in a name Halo recognized, Kimberly Henderson. The WWDS had her listed as one of the blue ribbon dog handlers and the payments coincided with the thefts. As a handler, Ms. Henderson would never be questioned about leaving with a dog.

Halo quickly made copies of all the documents and tucked them into her bag. With all this incriminating evidence, the Western Washington Dog Shows President would be able to question Ms. Henderson and hopefully she'd incriminate Pemsky.

After Halo put all the files back, she heard the front office door open. Crap, why hadn't she locked the door? On her next assignment she'd need a checklist to include the obvious: lock the door when you're rifling through things you're not supposed to. She stepped out of Pemsky's office and walked to her desk.

Mr. Pemsky stood in the reception area, his face the color of freshly cut beets.

"What the hell were you doing in my office, girly?" he demanded.

"Nothing... I'm just straightening things up for you. What are you doing out of the hospital? You should sit down. You don't look very good."

He stomped his foot and sweat dripped from his face.

"I'm fine and I'll take care of my office. Stay the hell out of there," he said with a huff.

He pushed Halo out of his way and her stupid heel caught on the carpet again and this time she couldn't catch herself. She fell and hit the back of her her head on the wall. "Ow!"

Talk about seeing stars.

Pemsky shook his head at her. He didn't even look her way as he walked into his office. She tried to get up, but her head spun.

Two minutes later, he stormed back out of his office. She still sat on the floor with her head in her hands, trying to muffle the pounding.

"Did you get into my files?" he yelled.

"No. I straightened your desk and moved your chair back," she calmly replied.

He panted and sweated profusely, and used the wall for support. Halo didn't want him to collapse on her. She turned to the side and tried to lift herself up on her knees, but he reached down and grabbed the lapel of her jacket and shook her.

"You stupid girl. Stay out of my office or you'll regret the day you were born. If I find out you're lying to me, I'll come looking for you. Do you understand?" Pemsky threatened.

"Yes... yes... I understand." She nodded even though the motion hurt her head.

He let go of her and clutched his chest, her cue to scramble to her feet. He terrified her and she didn't want him to think she'd be back in the morning.

"Mr. Pemsky, I was offered a permanent job. I left my resignation and keys to the office on your desk." Without looking in his direction, Halo grabbed her belongings and walked to the door. Before she could leave she heard movement behind her and cringed.

"Missy, you come over here. I want to take a look in that bag of yours."

"I'm sorry, I don't feel well. I'm going home now," she said, and quickly walked out of the office. She looked back then, but the door remained closed.

The stairs weren't an option with a band of psychotic drummers performing a jam session in her skull. She waited anxiously as the elevator displayed the numbers for each floor. A ding finally announced the elevator's arrival.

The doors opened and Rich stepped out of the elevator and blocked her escape route, with what smelled like a pepperoni pizza. She put her hand on his chest and pushed. Her wide-eyed look must've given him a hint that something could be wrong because he easily moved back into the elevator. The door closed and she moved away from him and slumped against the wall. The drummers were still having a party in her head.

"Halo, are you okay? What's going on?"

Halo needed to pull herself together and get the files back to Green Hornet Investigations. And her head could use a couple ibuprofens to kill the pain, which she had in the old medal ashtray in her Bug.

"Halo, talk to me," Rich insisted.

"I'm fine… everything's fine." She tried to sound convincing.

"You don't look fine. You look rattled."

"What are you doing here?" The pizza box in his hand told her everything she needed to know, but she didn't want to explain what happened.

"I took a chance you'd still be here, and brought you dinner."

"That was nice of you, but I've got to get going." Halo pushed the lobby button a few more times—not that it would make the box go any faster, but it felt good.

"You don't have time for dinner?" he asked.

"No. Sorry. How's Cleo? Did she have her pups?" She chose a safe topic.

"No, another false alarm. I'll probably take her to work with me tomorrow. I have a large staff that adores her and can watch over her for me while I work."

Halo had never ridden in an elevator that took this long to motor up and down. Finally, they arrived at the lobby.

"Thank you for thinking of me, but I can't stay." She maneuvered around his large body and smelled pepperoni and cheese. Her stomach protested her leaving with a loud gurgle.

"Are you sure? This is the best pizza ever; you'll be missing out," he said, and flaunted the box in front of her nose.

"Rich, I need to concentrate on my career right now. What I wish for and what I can have are two different things. I'm sorry."

He chuckled, but looked disappointed. She left him in the lobby, hitched her bag up over her shoulder, and walked the two blocks to the garage.

****

Rich couldn't believe his luck. The one girl that intrigued *him* wasn't interested in a relationship. Helen, his ex-wife had said she wanted a family, but after two years it became clear she preferred her fourteen-hour days at the office over coming home to their ten acres. When she insisted they sell the acreage and move to the city, he resisted and she divorced him.

Halo seemed sweet, kind, and passionate. Being a tenacious guy, he'd come back with food, but she'd

111

blown him off. Seriously, who could resist a pepperoni pizza from Josh's Pub?

When he heard the elevator ding and he didn't turn to see who got off. The guy walked by him with his shoulders slumped then turned, and stopped.

"Hey, I know you. You're the guy that called for the paramedics," Pemsky said.

He didn't want to talk to the guy—especially after the way he'd spoken to Halo.

"Yes, that was me." Pemsky looked worse now than he did earlier. His hands shook and sweat dripped down the side of his face.

"Did you see where that conniving receptionist went?"

"Excuse me, your receptionist saved your life," Rich reminded him.

"She didn't save my life. I had indigestion is all. So, where'd that girly go?" Pemsky demanded.

"I believe she went home, after a very long day at the office. Are you sure indigestion is your only health problem? Do you want me to call someone for you?" Rich asked.

"No. Mind your own business."

Pemsky leaned back against the wall and wiped his brow with his sleeve.

"Why do you need to find her?" Rich asked.

"I want to talk to her about something, not that's it any of your business," he replied, with a sneer on his face.

"Whatever you need, I'm sure that it can wait until tomorrow." Rich turned to leave.

"She quit, dammit! She walked out on me without notice," he said with a huff.

Spittle formed in the corners of his mouth.

"Well, goodbye and take care." Rich left Pemsky in the lobby of the building.

Curiosity plagued Rich. Halo acted nervous in the elevator. Could Pemsky be the reason? Halo had at least a fifteen minute head start, but it couldn't hurt to drive around. He might get lucky. She hadn't looked his way when she drove by the front of the building, but he recognized her in a lemon-yellow Bug.

He'd only gone four blocks when he spotted puffs of blue smoke coming from under the hood of her car in a supermarket parking lot. She looked defeated with an empty jug of water in her hand.

He parked his car and got out. She didn't notice him at first. She kicked the tires and mumbled something about taking "Sunshine" to the junkyard.

"Halo, looks like Sunshine needs more than a little water to fix her," he said, and watched her eyes go from frightened to relieved, in a split second.

"You keep turning up in unexpected places. Were you following me?" she asked with suspicion in her voice, and closed the hood of her car.

"No. I hoped I'd run into you again though. Speaking of running into someone, Mr. Pemsky wasn't too happy that you quit your job. What happened?" Rich waited for her to respond.

"My assignment's almost over so I can tell you I work undercover for Green Hornet Investigations. The Western Washington Dog Show suspected Pemsky of stealing pedigree dogs and then selling them back to their owners. I found the records implicating him and one of the dog handlers."

"Pemsky sounds like an unscrupulous guy. You better be careful."

"I know and he has a terrible temper," Halo said and looked around.

"You can't go to the police with these files because you copied them without Pemsky's permission. What are you going to do with them?"

"The President of WWDS will do the investigation, not us. Their organization is a tight knit group of people and wants to handle this internally— whatever that means."

"As long as Pemsky doesn't figure out you were involved. I have a feeling he suspects something, though."

"I know. He's a pretty scary guy. When he thought I'd been in his office, he shook me a little."

"What do you mean he *shook* you?" Rich's temper simmered at the thought of Pemsky hurting Halo.

"High heels are hard to get used to. I tripped, hit my head, and he grabbed me when I was already on the floor."

"Halo, let me see it. Why didn't you tell me earlier?" He gently ran his hand over a good size lump on her head.

"It's just a bump on the head. I'll be fine."

He wanted to throttle Pemsky.

"I need to get these files to Corny, my boss. Unfortunately, my car went capoot on me. I hate to ask, but can you give me a lift? My office isn't far from here."

"Yes, of course. So... you're a private investigator?" That's the last profession he would've pictured Halo in.

"Well, I'm more like a pet detective in training," Halo explained.

Rich opened the passenger door, took her bag, and laid it on the seat. He moved a step closer, wanting another taste of her lips. He pressed his body into hers, holding her tight against the side of the car.

"What are you doing?" she whispered.

She put her hands on his chest. He didn't think she intended to push him away.

"Just one taste," he said as he lowered his head and softly kissed her beautiful lips. He didn't want to rush her, so he rested his forehead against hers. After a moment, he studied her soulful eyes. She had moisture building, ready to spill over.

"You have the most beautiful eyes. Why do they look sad?"

"Bad timing is all," she said and looked away.

"Okay, I'll slow down. Climb in. Which direction are we headed?" he asked, to lighten the mood.

"Green Hornet Investigations is off of Second Avenue near Green Lake. I should call Corny and let her know what happened, but my phone's dead. I hate it when I forget to charge the darn thing."

He handed Halo his phone. "Use mine."

"Are you sure?"

"Make your phone call, Halo."

"I really appreciate your help. Thank you." She sniffed the air and turned around in her seat. "Boy, that pizza smells good."

"I haven't had a chance to eat a bite yet." He heard Halo's stomach growl and grinned at her. "There are napkins in the glove compartment. Please, help yourself."

Out of the corner of his eye, he saw Halo touch the back of her head and wince. Then she made the phone call.

"Corny, I've got the evidence. I'll be at the office in five minutes. Great. See you then."

She handed the phone back to him, turned around, and selected a small slice. After eating a couple bites, she put the remainder back in the box and closed the lid.

"Thank you. That's great pizza, but my stomach can't handle much more."

"How's your head?" he asked.

"The throbbing has lessened to a thump-thump."

"Do you have someone to take care of you, like a roommate, ex-husband, dog or cat?"

"No roommate and definitely no ex-husband. Someday, I'll have a couple acres of land. I want tons of critters: goats, pigs, ducks, chickens, cats, dogs, and maybe even a turkey. I just need to focus on my career first, and eventually I'll have all that."

It sounded as though she loved animals as much as he did.

"People are always bringing me their unwanted animals. I have plenty to spare if you want to adopt a few," he joked.

"Maybe in a few months, when I'll have a large enough place to keep them."

She raised her hand and pointed up ahead.

"See that big green sign on the right? You can drop me off there."

"Halo, you don't have to give up a career to have a relationship—or pets, for that matter."

She didn't say anything. She didn't even acknowledge what he'd said. He pulled over in front of Green Hornet Investigations. Before he could ask for her phone number, she'd hopped out of the car, but leaned back in before he could move.

"Thank you for everything. I hope Cleo has her puppies soon."

He got of the driver's side and said, "Hey, wait. I want to see you again. We can work around your schedule."

"Rich, you're a great guy. I just don't have time right now for anybody or anything in my life. Thank you again for all your help today," she said and looked away.

Were those tears on her cheek? If so, then why didn't she want to see him again? If only she'd give him a chance, she might be able to have everything she ever wanted. He'd never understand women.

❖Chapter Three❖

A week later

Ms. Henderson came forward and revealed the dog theft scheme she and Mr. Pemsky had been involved in. She said he came up with the scheme and insisted she'd been an unwilling accomplice. The public became outraged and wanted Pemsky's head on a dog platter. Mr. Pemsky's face showed up on every news station bruised, and defeated. The WWDS must've exacted their revenge shortly before his apprehension.

❖Chapter Four❖

Three months later

A week before Christmas, three inches of pristine white snow fell during the night. The weather forecaster promised the snow would continue to fall through the New Year. What could be better than that?

After Sunshine died a smoky death, Halo used the Seattle transit system. The bus might've been cheaper, but cramped her style and slowed down her pet retrievals.

Early that morning, Corny sent her out to find the Smith's missing beagle, Henry. The owners believed one of their creepy neighbors grabbed him out of their backyard while he did his business. Mr. Smith said the neighbors always complained about Henry's barking, which turned out to be a byproduct of the neighbors yelling at each other.

The bus dropped Halo off a block from the Smith's house and she did a hard-target search—she looked in an alley and behind a couple shops. Halo spotted a beagle hunkered down in front of a mini-mart. People didn't usually leave their pets outside for long in thirty degree weather, so that had to be Henry, but she went inside and asked anyway.

"Hey, do you know who owns the dog out front?" Halo asked.

"Huh? What dog?" the pimpled-faced teenager asked.

"The beagle out front? Do you know who owns him?" she enunciated with care.

"Sorry. I don't know nothin about no dog."

Henry howled and the kid jumped.

"Dude, was that, like, a werewolf?" he asked.

The kid looked around, as though he expected a hairy, fanged wolf to appear.

"No, that's just Henry." Halo said, and left the kid looking around nervously in his low-rider jeans.

She squatted down in front of the beagle. His whole body shook from the cold.

"Henry, I'll get you home soon, but we'll have to take the bus. Here, let me put these little wool booties on your feet. I knitted them myself."

Halo crisscrossed her large bag over her head and under her arm and lifted Henry. Wow, twenty-five pounds of dog felt like fifty. The bus driver refused to let Henry on at first, but all the seats were empty, so he changed his mind—all in the Christmas spirit.

❖Chapter Five❖

Halo socked away a nice chunk of change for a future gently used car, but she'd received a huge Christmas surprise. Her parents decided to visit a few days before Christmas and looked immaculate as always—her dad in Armani and her mom in Calvin Klein and pearls.

Her mom kissed Halo's cheek and took her hand in hers.

"Darling, Halo," her mom gushed. "We're so proud of what you've accomplished this year. You've really found your niche in life. All those other jobs were just a prequel to your becoming a pet detective. Corny told us that you rescued a sweet beagle and returned him using the transit system. How resourceful."

"Well, I didn't have a choice but to use the bus, because Sunshine died," she explained.

"I know, dear. I'm so sorry. You loved that pretty little yellow car. Honey, your little home looks very festive. The tea lights give off such a warm glow to your little home. Oh, and what beautiful doilies."

Halo watched her mom as she glanced around the apartment. Yes, her apartment could be considered small, but the studio had her style written all over the place.

From the tiny, live Christmas tree in the corner, to the blinking, large colored lights hung around her windows.

"I made the dollies, the curtains, and the sofa cover myself," Halo volunteered to fill the awkward silence.

"They're lovely, darling."

"Well... I hope you're hungry. I have a fresh turkey breast in the oven and I've made cornbread stuffing, mashed sweet potatoes and gravy—just like we had when I was a kid. I made a batch of spritz cookies for dessert, too," she said, getting into the whole family get-together spirit. Who could resist spritz cookies with red and green sprinkles? Not her.

Her dad looked uncomfortable, and her mom spoke up.

"Oh, that's what smells so scrumptious. You've always been creative. I'm not sure where you got that trait from—not me. I'm sorry, darling. We can't stay for dinner. Your Dad and I have a plane to catch in a couple hours. We're spending the holidays with the Krutcher's in the Bahamas this year."

"Are you sure you can't stay for dinner?" Halo asked.

"Sorry, we're in such a rush this year."

Cripes, she'd be eating turkey leftovers through the New Year.

"Why don't you come downstairs and we'll show you your Christmas present," her mom said with excitement in her voice.

"My present is downstairs?" Halo would've' loved an hour with her parents over a present anyway.

122

"Come see for yourself."

Halo's mom took her hand and led her to the door. Her parents were definitely in a hurry to leave. She loved her parents, but their expectations were much higher for her than she could ever achieve. Having a cardiologist and a pediatrician for parents put pressure on Halo to be something great, like a brain surgeon but she hated the sight of blood.

Halo grabbed her hand-knitted blue hat, blue gloves, and wool coat, and then trucked down to the curb in front of her building. She wondered what they'd come up with this year? She usually received savings bonds, which she'd cash in to pay her rent.

In a dramatic gesture, her mom spread her arms wide, indicating Halo should look at the car sitting in front of them.

"Halo, darling, your dad and I thought you'd appreciate a new car over savings bonds this year. What do you think? I made sure the Honda was a nice bright yellow."

"This...this is mine? You bought me a car?" Halo looked from her mom to her dad and they both nodded. The four-door Honda had all-weather tires, fabric interior, and an automatic transmission. Perfect. She'd have wheels again.

Halo gave both her parents bearhugs, not caring that she got their perfectly tailored clothes wet.

"Thank you, Mom and Dad. The Honda is wonderful... perfect and incredibly generous. I wish you didn't have to leave so soon," Halo said and meant it.

"Oh honey, we'll get together after the holidays and you can tell us all about your pet adventures," her mom said, and kissed Halo on the cheek.

"Now, take care of that car. We're not buying you another one," Halo's dad said as he headed toward his car. He turned—teary eyed and said, "I'm proud of you, honey."

"I love you both," Halo said, and wiped her eyes.

"We love you, too," they said in unison.

Before they pulled away, Halo saw her mom kiss her dad on the cheek. She hopped up and down in the snow and then climbed into her new car and took the yellow bullet for a spin.

In the last couple months, she'd driven by Rich's vet clinic, hoping to get a glimpse of him. She couldn't do that in a bus, but in her new car she circled twice. She wondered if he'd done the same.

❖Chapter Six❖

Rich tried to curb his anger for the human race by clenching his fist. Who would leave a cloth diaper bag with two kittens in the middle of a busy road? Fortunate for the little ones, a young man pulled over and checked the bag before squashing them under the tires of his Ford pickup. Not knowing what to do with the hungry, cold kittens the good Samaritan brought them to the closest veterinarian office—his. They were adorable, like all kittens. They looked like siblings, with short, multi-colored tabby fur and blue eyes. He named them Tick and Tack. Another couple animals wouldn't be a problem to add to the McFarland ranch—unless he could find another animal lover to care for them?

Halo… he'd never stopped thinking about her. Three months passed. Would she still be on a dating break or did she already have a boyfriend? He got a brilliant idea. He'd ask Halo to find out who left the kittens in the middle of the road. They could have lunch together and then maybe dinner and then who knew? Of course, he wouldn't return the kittens if she found the owners, but he would report the abuse to the Humane Society.

Green Hornet Investigations wasn't far from his clinic. He'd driven by her office several times, always hoping to spot her. Tick and Tack liked riding in his SUV. They sat in their carrier like little troopers. He'd seat-belted their carrier in the front seat so he could stroke their tiny heads when he stopped. He hated to use animals as leverage, but they'd give him an edge with Halo.

She could be with family, since Christmas would arrive in only two days. He'd find out soon enough. He arrived and unbuckled Tick and Tack from the seat while snow dumped from the sky in a solid sheet. At the last minute, he covered their carrier with a small blanket. "Come on cuties; let's go charm the pants off Halo."

The door chimed *coo coo*, like the sound of doves and the cheerful receptionist greeted him with warmth.

"Merry Christmas! How may I help you?" she asked with a big grin on her face.

"Hi. Merry Christmas to you, too. My name's Rich McFarland and I wonder if Halo is available," he asked as he lowered the kittens to the ground. The receptionist eye's followed the carrier. She extended her hand for a shake.

"Hi, I'm Brenda. Halo's aunt. She's out right now. Can I help you with something?"

Meow...meow.

"Whatcha got there?" Brenda came out from around her desk and knelt down to look in the carrier.

Meow...meow.

"Oh... how cute. Corny, come out here. You've gotta see these little kittens. What are their names?" Brenda asked.

"The one with the white speck on her head is Tick and her brother is Tack. They were found in the middle of the road and brought to my clinic," Rich explained.

A beautiful, smiling redhead came out of an office in the back, dressed in red from head-to-toe, her earrings blinked when she walked.

"Hi, I'm Corny. You're a vet, huh? Halo told me she met a nice vet a couple months ago. Was that you?" she asked, and squatted down next to the kittens, too.

"We did meet a couple months ago. I'm hoping I'm the one she spoke of."

She stuck her finger in a slit in the plastic carrier and Tick batted at her.

"They're darling," Corny said.

Corny tilted her head and looked up at him. He stuck his hand out a second time. "I'm Rich."

"Nice to meet you. What can we do for you?" she asked.

Brenda jumped in and answered for him.

"Rich is looking for Halo. Do you know when she'll be back, Corny?"

Tack stuck his paw through the slit and took a playful swipe at Brenda too. She giggled.

Before Corny could answer, her cell rang. She checked the caller ID and then smiled at him. After a moment she closed her eyes, and took a deep breath. When she opened them again her mouth formed a hard line.

"What's wrong?" Brenda asked.

"Call Steve. Tell him Pemsky is out of jail and is playing bumper cars with Halo, and that I'm going after her."

"You need to call the police," Rich said, as he watched Corny gather her purse and keys.

"My boyfriend is a cop," Corny declared.

"Maybe you should wait for him," Brenda said.

"She won't be alone, Brenda," he said, and asked Corny."What do you drive?"

"A Mini Cooper. Why?"

"Because the snow is coming down thick as a blanket. I have an SUV that'll get us to Halo faster and safer."

"Please call me as soon as you know something. I'm scared. What if she's hurt bad?" Brenda said.

Brenda's tears ran down her face. Corny looked fierce.

"We'll take care of her. Let's go, Rich," Corny said.

"How far away is she?" he asked.

"About thirty minutes. Her phone went dead and she's not picking up her phone. God, she has to be okay."

She better be, or he'd ring Pemsky's neck.

❖Chapter Seven❖

Of course, Halo chose the day before Christmas Eve, a night when the snowflakes were as big as quarters, to make the drive out to her friend's house. She felt melancholy and wanted to see Sue's cow, Henrietta. She'd birthed a calf and Halo wanted to stroke the little creature. Besides, they'd invited her for dinner and she didn't want to eat anymore leftovers.

She'd thought a lot about Rich over the last couple months and wondered where he'd spend the holidays. Did he already have a girlfriend? Probably. Who wouldn't snag an available, nice, good-looking guy who loved animals?

Stop being a baby. You're the one who told him you were too busy with your job to spend time with him.

She looked in her rear-view mirror for the third time. While she sat there feeling sorry for herself, the car behind her inched closer. Jeez, could they get any closer to her bumper without making contact? She slowed down and pulled over to the right in case they wanted to pass. She waved them on, but the car wouldn't pass her. What could be the problem? Were they drunk or on drugs?

When the car made the last left-hand turn, right behind her, still tailgating, her worry increased and perspiration formed under her arms. The large, dark sedan had been right behind her for the last twenty minutes. Halo gripped the steering wheel looking ahead at the deserted road, except for scattered farms.

In the blink of an eye, the sedan accelerated and pulled up beside her. What a stupid move, with this limited visibility. She held tight to the steering wheel, but the car didn't pass. The window lowered and a finger extended her way. She lowered hers, confused. Then she recognized Pemsky's nasty sneer. The snow felt like ice pellets as they blasted her face.

"Mr. Pemsky, what are you doing?" Halo screamed over the road noise.

"You stupid little girl. Did you think I wouldn't want payback for what you did to me? You ruined my business, my wife left me, and I lost everything because of you. You're going to pay for what you did to me," he yelled back.

"I didn't do anything. You should be ashamed of yourself for stealing those dogs."

Pemsky threw back his head and laughed. He yanked the wheel and veered toward her. With quick reflexes, she swerved to her right. Her Civic hit the shoulder and spun up gravel.

Oh shit!

Halo raised her window while she fumbled for her cell and dialed Corny, who picked up after the first ring.

"Hi Halo. Merry Christmas," Corny said in a cheerful voice.

130

"Pemsky is trying to run me off the road. I didn't know he got out of jail," Halo sobbed. She wiped her nose on her sleeve and tried to keep her car on the road.

"Where are you?" Corny asked.

"I'm out on Route 25, about ten minutes from Sue's farmhouse."

"I'm on my way. I'll have Brenda call Sue and tell her what's going on. You'll have people coming to the rescue from both directions. Now, don't hang up," Corny insisted.

"Okay. Hurry…"

Pemsky rolled up his window and his car lurched over the middle line again. Halo held tight to the steering wheel but her cell slipped from her fingers and fell to the floor. He swerved back into his lane and she tapped her brakes. If she had to make a run for the field, she would.

Pemsky slowed his car too and slammed into the front corner of her car. The side of Halo's head hit and bounced off the driver's window. "Ow, ow!"

Screech… screech…

Panic and pain caused Halo to hit the brakes harder then she should have. She skidded sidewise but got her car to stop. Her vision blurred. The Civic now sat in the middle of the country road. Her door had caved in a couple inches from the impact. She'd need to crawl over to the passenger's door to get out.

She shook herself. No! She needed to get to the farmhouse, if she wanted to survive. She pushed down on the gas pedal and the tires spun and then grabbed.

Pemsky caught up with her, honked his horn twice, and drove his car into the back quarter panel. This time, she lost control.

Around and around she spun.

All of a sudden, her life flashed before her eyes. Why did it take her life to be in danger for her to understand what's truly important in life—love! She wanted to go out on a date with Rich, pet his dog Cleo, and cuddle her puppies. Halo wanted everything…

Then the lights went out.

Once on the road, Rich drove as fast as the conditions would allow him, which wasn't fast enough for him. Corny sat silently beside him with hands clutched in her lap. Corny got ahold of Sue, and she and her husband Jack were headed in Halo's direction. She said they'd call when they reached her.

Steve, Corny's boyfriend called and they talked for a couple minutes. Rich took her short replies, 'sorry', 'I know', 'sorry',' I know', to mean Steve wasn't happy she'd left without him.

When Corny's cell rang again, she jumped.

"Oh God, no… Did you call for the paramedics? Okay…okay. We're almost there. No, don't move her. Did you bring blankets? Good, keep her warm. We'll be there soon. Thank you for being there for her."

Corny hung up, blew her nose, and wiped her eyes.

"What? Tell me!" Rich demanded. He watched her take a deep breath.

"Halo's car's on its side in the ditch. She's unconscious. The paramedics are on the way."

"Do your friends know how bad she's hurt?" Rich asked.

"Sue said her ankle looks like it's pinned under the dash of her car, but she's not sure how badly she's hurt. Drive faster, Rich."

Corny fumbled with her cell, and gave Steve an update, which seemed to calm her. He pulled around a bend in the road and slowed at the sight before them. Only half of a bright yellow Honda Civic could be seen; the rest was in a large ditch. A green pickup truck sat over on the side of the road. Jack and Sue, he hoped.

"Rich..." Corny whispered.

"I know. I know. She's going to be fine," he said in a reassuring voice. "She has to be."

He parked and they ran over to the ditch. Jake had the car window covered, to keep the warmth in and snow out, and they'd covered Halo in blankets. He could see dried blood on her temple and her leg wedged under the dashboard. He crawled down into the ditch and gently took her hand. Her skin felt cold to the touch. He bent down as far as he could and rubbed his cheek against hers. "Baby, you're going to be okay. I promise."

He could hear the sirens in the distance.

Hurry.

❖Chapter Eight❖

Halo rubbed her cheek against something warm and a little bit rough, and smelled wonderful. Realization dawned, along with pain—everywhere.

"Ohh," she whispered. Her voice sounded far away and her throat hurt.

"Come on, Halo. Open your eyes for me, baby," Rich said.

Rich? How did he get here? Halo tried to open her eyes, but the overhead lights were bright and made her head pound. She managed to open one eye and looked around.

"Where am I?" she croaked.

"You're in the emergency room at Joseph's Hospital. Are you thirsty?"

Halo nodded. That seemed to be easier than talking. Rich slipped a straw between her lips.

"Ahh... Thank you. That feels good. What are you doing here?"

"I missed you and didn't want to wait any longer to see you. I stopped by your office and happened to be there when you called Corny," he replied and stroked her forehead.

"I'm glad you're here." She tried to move her legs but her left leg felt like lead. She panicked.

"Rich, how come I can't move my leg?" She clasped Rich's hand as hard as she could.

"Your foot is fine, Halo. Your ankle sustained a hairline fracture in the wreck and they put your leg in a plaster cast to protect it. I promise you'll be good as new in no time."

He kissed her forehead. Then her memory returned in a flood. "Where's Pemsky? He ran me off the road. He said he'd get payback for what I did. What if he shows up here?"

"Calm down, honey. Pemsky won't *ever* bother you again," Rich reassured her.

"Was he arrested?" Halo needed to know before she could relax. Her heart rate increased and the monitors bleeped in tune.

Before Rich could answer, the hospital curtain parted and Brenda, Corny, and Steve, quietly walked in. Rich stepped away as they crowded around her bed.

"You scared the begeezees out of us, Halo," Brenda said, and dabbed her eyes with her knuckle.

"Yeah, I'm the only one who's allowed to get hurt around here," Corny joked.

"I disagree. *No one* needs to get hurt," Steve insisted.

Corny introduced Rich to Steve and they shook hands. Rich stepped forward and took her hand.

"I'm in agreement with Steve," Rich said.

"Somebody please tell me where Pemsky is," Halo insisted.

"I will," Brenda said, and leaned forward. "There was a freak accident and Pemsky died."

"That's it? That's all you're going to tell me?" Halo croaked. Rich slipped a straw between her lips again and she sucked.

"Honey, are you sure you want to hear this now? Why don't we wait until you're feeling better," Brenda suggested.

"No, I want to hear what happened now, before I go home." Panic set in. "I can go home, right? I don't want to spend the holidays here."

Brenda looked at Corny and Steve and they gave her a small nod.

"Sweetie, the hospital said they'd release you today. That's good news," Brenda said.

"Stop trying to protect me and tell me what's going on," Halo said, as she looked around at everyone.

Rich kissed her hand and rubbed her knuckles with his thumb. She felt safe. The heart monitor slowed to a steady beat.

"Now, tell me about Pemsky. Please," Halo said, and looked at Rich.

"I'll tell you what the state trooper's concluded from their preliminary investigation. Pemsky sped away after he ran you off the road. They approximated his speed to be around seventy-five miles per hour when he took a sharp curve and swerved to miss a couple cows in the road. His car broke through a wire fence and collided with a tractor. The cause of death was determined to be by John Deere."

"Oh my... Oh my.... How horrible. His poor family," Halo said. Everyone else kept silent. "Are the cows okay?"

136

"Yes, he missed the cows," Rich replied, and everyone laughed.

Halo looked at the clock across the hall as the dial hit midnight, which made it Christmas Eve. Tears slipped from her eyes.

"Halo, you're going to be on crutches for six weeks and won't be able to manage stairs very well, which I'm told you only have at your apartment. You'll need to stay with someone who can care for you for a little while. Brenda's volunteered, until you can get around on your own."

"Okay, I can deal with that." Halo looked at her aunt. "Are you going to be okay taking care of an invalid?"

"Yes, honey. We'll have a grand time," Brenda replied.

"We'll go get Halo's crutches and meds and leave you two alone for a minute," Brenda said, and everyone but Rich left the cubicle.

"Honey, everything will be all right," Rich said, and kissed her.

"I feel bad. It's Christmas Eve and everyone is stuck here at the hospital with me."

"Halo, that's what people do when they love someone."

"When I was spinning out of control, I realized how I cheated both of us by thinking I couldn't have a career and a relationship, too."

"We have all the time in the world, Halo."

❖ Chapter Nine ❖

Christmas Eve

By 8:00 a.m. all the essentials Halo would need for the next couple weeks were collected from her apartment and organized in Brenda's spare bedroom. Even the Christmas presents she'd handmade for everyone sat under the tree.

With the crisis now over, Steve and Corny headed to her parent's house. Brenda and John had a quiet Christmas planned, which meant she hadn't screwed up too much of their holiday. Everyone looked bushed, though.

Rich stayed around and helped get her situated at Brenda's. When Rich got ready to leave, Brenda handed him a small animal carrier. The mariachi band in her head stopped her from asking any questions. After making a trip to his car, Rich came over to the couch and kissed her with such tenderness; it brought tears to her eyes.

"Would you like to spend Christmas with me? Brenda said it would be okay with her," Rich asked.

"Can you cook?" He'd gotten the deer-in-the-headlights look—priceless. He recovered quickly with a smile.

"That depends on who you ask. Don't you worry; I'll make sure we have a turkey and all the trimmings."

"I'd love to. What time do you want me to come over?"

"Halo, you can't drive. I'll pick you up at noon. You've had a rough couple of days. Sleep well and I'll see you in the morning, Sunshine," Rich said, and kissed her again before he left.

Halo didn't know Rich well enough to buy him a present, but she thought it would be okay to buy Cleo, his dog, something. Brenda made a late-night trip to Walmart and bought a dozen dog toys and a loaf of garlic bread. If the Turkey burnt they could munch on bread.

She'd slept late Christmas morning due to the pain-killers. Crutches and a leg-cast made getting in and out of the shower and dressed a slow process. She had to hurry to be ready on time. She'd managed to wrap the doggy toys, but after that her body complained.

The door bell rang exactly at noon. Brenda answered the door in her bright red Santa sweater and hat.

"Merry Christmas, Rich. Come in. Would you like a glass of eggnog?" Brenda asked.

She'd already had two and her eyes looked glassy and bright, Halo noticed.

"Merry Christmas to you, too. No thank you, on the eggnog." He looked at Halo and asked, "How are you feeling? Are you still up for coming over?"

"Yes. I can't wait. I'm looking forward to seeing Cleo and her pups. Maybe you, too." Brenda left them alone and Rich wrapped her in his arms and kissed the socks off her.

"You taste wonderful," Rich said, with huskiness in his voice.

"You do too." Halo felt her face growing warm.

"Let's get you in the car. There are already a couple of inches of snow on the ground and the weather forecaster predicted another couple by tonight. We're definitely having a white Christmas."

Rich sounded excited. When he picked her up she squealed. "What are you doing?"

"Honey, the snow is slick. I'd hate for you to fall. I'm going to carry you to the car."

"Sorry, the pain meds make me stupid."

"You? Stupid? I don't think so." He emphasized his point with gentle kisses to her lips, then picked up her bag and looped the handles around his neck

Brenda walked in to say goodbye.

"You two have a wonderful Christmas. See you tonight, honey," Brenda said, with eggnog cheer in her voice.

The drive to Rich's house only took twenty minutes. Not a lot of people were out and about on Christmas day. He drove down a long dirt road and they stopped in front of an old farmhouse. The white house with yellow shutters and a beautiful wraparound porch shone with little white lights. They wove through a Christmas wreath on the front door, around the railing, and the length of the porch. He even had a porch swing with green and red-stripped cushions.

"Oh… What a great house," Halo exclaimed.

Out of the corner of her eye, she spotted a dozen or so chickens pecking the ground, looking for food under the snow. As Rich got out of the car, a large yellow lab came to greet them. He jumped, wiggled, jumped, and wiggled some more until Rich gave him a big hug.

"Now you stay down, Sam."

The dog obeyed. Rich wrapped Halo's bag around his neck and carried her to the porch where he set her on the swing.

"I need to do one more thing before you can come in. Will you be all right for a couple minutes?"

"Of course. Can Sam sit on the swing with me?"

Sam wiggled his rear end in excitement, his tail flying back and forth.

"I can tell you're going to spoil my pets. Okay, but only because it's Christmas. Sam, up," he commanded.

Sam responded with a gentle leap and licked her hand.

"Take your time. Sam and I are going to get acquainted."

Halo heard a commotion inside the house, but stayed put. All of a sudden she heard a door slam, cursing, and around the side of the house, came another dog and a half dozen puppies yipping their little hearts out. Sam jumped down and the dogs wrestled in the snow. Playful growls erupted from the bunch.

Rich opened the front door, sat down next to Halo, and took her hand in his.

"Welcome to the McFarland Zoo."

"How many and what kinds of pets do you have?" she asked, with awe in her voice.

"I've lost track, but I love them all."

Halo could tell he did.

"Let's get you warm. I tried to wrap your Christmas presents, but they aren't cooperating."

"They?"

"Yes, *they*…" he laughed.

What a wonderful sound. Rich carried her into the house and lowered her down on the couch.

"I'll be right back," he said, and walked down a hallway.

Meow…meow!

Rich walked toward her with a small box. The lip popped open and two kittens crawled up the sides. He grabbed them before they fell to the floor.

"Merry Christmas," he said, with a grin on his face.

The kittens jumped out of his arms, landed on her lap, circled, kneaded her with their paws and fell asleep.

"They're mine?" Halo stroked their heads and a rumble erupted from both of them.

"Yes, if you'll have them," he said and laughed.

"They're beautiful. What are their names?"

"Tick and Tack. They were rescued and brought to my office. And I have something to confess."

"Go ahead." Halo couldn't keep her hands off their soft fur.

"I was going to use them to get a date with you. I brought them by your office as an excuse to see you, but then things fell apart."

"You're shameless, but I'm so happy you did."

"Open your present now." Halo pointed to a large box on the table. "I wasn't sure what to get you. I hope this is okay."

Rich slipped his finger under the tape holding the paper closed and stopped.

"Just as long as the present isn't alive," he joked and continued to unwrap his present. "Wow. How great! Dog toys. We think alike."

They leaned toward each other and shared a long, hot, holiday kiss, as the dogs roared into the living room. The kittens woke up, hissed, and swatted at the dogs.

Halo's stomach grumbled and rumbled. Reminding her she hadn't eaten a decent meal since leaving for Sue's. "Do you need help with dinner? I like to cook. I can help."

"Sure. Let me go shoot the turkey and you can sit here and pluck his feathers," he said with a straight face.

"What? We have to kill our dinner?" Halo asked in shock.

He chuckled and shook his head.

"Oh, Halo, I'm just kidding. My neighbor is cooking dinner for us. She'll deliver the feast in about twenty minutes."

"You had me there for a minute," she said.

He leaned forward, took her face in his hands, and kissed her. When they moved apart he rested his forehead against hers. He looked up, as though he'd just remembered something.

"Did I tell you, I have a pig named, Ziggy?"

"You… you… have a pig? Named, Ziggy? I've always wanted a pig," Halo said, with longing.

143

His smile turned into a huge grin.

"Oh my sweet, Halo. Ziggy will love you."

Rich leaned over and kissed the sensitive spot above Halo's collarbone. She moaned. He moved to the other sensitive spot behind her ear. Another moan escaped her lips.

"You like that?" he asked in a husky voice.

"More…" that's all Halo could manage.

Rich gave Halo more kisses, and soft touches. When she looked into his beautiful green eyes, she saw her future and everything she'd ever wanted.

The doorbell rang and the dogs barked, the kittens hissed, and she heard a *cocka-doodle-doo* in the distance.

WHAT A WONDERFUL CHRISTMAS!

A CHRISTMAS HOPE
CASEY DAWES

❖Chapter One❖

Clara Misowski was glued to the six o'clock evening news.

A man's craggy face, guarded by a thick, but trimmed, black beard reflected the stony countryside behind him. His wild locks blew in the chilly late November wind.

Heathcliff in the flesh.

Clara leaned forward on her couch. She ached to reach through the plasma and touch him to make sure he was real. His piercing eyes taunted her with their vibrancy.

Or insanity.

Maybe she was the crazy one. Longing after a man on television was a sign of true desperation.

Three failed businesses and an abortive marriage had made her doubt her ability to make a success of anything. Her latest venture—a tasting party and culinary road trip business she'd named The Perfect Plate—would be her last chance at independence. Her most recent bank statement had shown a pitifully small balance. If something didn't change soon, she'd need to get a job. The thought of working for someone else made her shudder.

When her husband had left her to move in with his secretary—*how clichéd is that?*—he'd made it clear he thought she didn't have anything to offer a *real* man. You're too flighty," he'd told her. "You can't keep house, can't run a business, and definitely can't keep a man satisfied in bed."

Clara glanced back at the man on the television. He looked like he'd never known a happy day in his life. He'd probably make her miserable.

Then why did she have a burning desire to meet him?

She must be certifiable. That was the only possible answer.

On the screen, the impeccably dressed reporter smiled at the camera. Her black leather coat and matching high heeled boots mocked Clara's sweats. The reporter's carefully painted lips enunciated her words. "Sam Richards is a fourth generation farmer from Duchess County in upstate New York."

While she spoke the unsmiling man stepped farther away from the reporter as if distancing himself from anything resembling fame.

"When he left for college, along with many of the young people from this small farming town of Roxbury," the reporter continued, "few expected him to come back home. But Sam Richards did return, a small sign that the brain drain from this charming, but rural, agricultural community may be reversing. Since his return, he's converted the family dairy farm to an artisan cheese-making operation."

A charming small town. Sounded like Clara's kind of place.

She grabbed a piece of paper, wrote down "Sam Richards," "cheese," and "Roxbury, NY," and went back to staring at the screen.

The camera followed the reporter as a black and white dog herded her toward Sam. When the dog successfully achieved its goal, it sat and waited for praise from its master.

Sam glanced at the dog, a hint of a smile softening the hard planes of his face, and patted its head.

"What made you decide to return?" the reporter asked before she thrust the microphone into Sam's face.

The man's features closed back down.

He hates this.

The reporter wiggled the microphone.

Sam shrugged. "I never bought the line of bull that a city's a better place to live, and an office job is the only career." He gestured to the sheep scattered across the meadow and the tree-covered mountains in the distance. "This is how people are supposed to live."

Sheep. He owns sheep. Why can't he make cheese from cows? Or even goats?

While the reporter closed the segment, Clara turned on her computer tablet and searched for "artisan cheese Roxbury NY." Halfway down the page, she saw what she was looking for: "Richards Handmade Cheese." His website was a bare-bones effort that explained how he made the cheese, and where she could buy it. The "About" section pictured Richards with his dog, but gave minimal information about the owner.

The company's phone number hid in tiny numerals at the bottom of the page.

No wife or partner was mentioned.

Heathcliff might be available.

She sighed. *I'm lusting after a man I don't know who obviously wants to be left alone.*

But it's late November—almost Christmas, her more optimistic self whispered. *Isn't that what the season is about? Hope that things will change? Maybe with the right tactics, I could convince him to rediscover the joy of the season.*

Clara searched the Internet for more information about the town. As her fingers slid, flicked, and tapped over the screen, she realized Roxbury would be a great place for her first long-distance tasting and shopping trip. Besides the handsome cheesemaker destined to break her heart, there was a winery, a farm with exotic animals, and a bed and breakfast with organic foodstuffs and local handcrafted items. Google Earth showed a farm-studded area hugging the rough contours of the Catskill Mountains. Once snow fell, the area would be Christmas card picturesque.

The owners of the winery and animal farm should be easily convinced to set up demonstrations for the clients of The Perfect Plate. Sam Richards might be a little more difficult.

Maybe if she showed up in person, she could persuade him. She could make the trip to Duchess County on Friday, right after her visit to her mom.

The impulse to visit Sam Richards galloped through her brain, while logic pulled at the reins. She ignored the tug of common sense.

Sam must need publicity because he'd done the interview with the New York television station. Clara would have to convince him that catering to her group would help him sell more cheese.

After tapping back to the cheesemaker's site, she pulled up the "Locations" page.

Good. King's carries his cheese.

Clara glanced at the time on the computer, flicked off the television, and walked to her bedroom to throw on a sweater and jeans, and run a brush through her hair. King's Grocers wasn't the corner store. Even at this late hour she might run into one of her wealthy clients. After sliding her favorite gloss over her lips, she dashed out the door.

At the market, she took her time and walked through all the aisles. Tangy vinegar odors from open bins of olives and pickles, yeasty smells of artisan breads, and a whiff of citrus from Clementine oranges, grapefruit, and lemons teased her nose. With only a few dollars in her pocket, rich smells would have to do.

Clara ended her tour of culinary delights at the cheese section. A short gray-haired woman with a thick European accent helped her find Richards Handmade Cheese. Clara selected three of the smallest pieces and made her way to the bargain bins where she snagged a cheap bottle of pinot noir and crusty day-old bread.

After she returned home with her purchases, she opened the wine to air, lay out her feast, put on classical music, and sat at her kitchen table to sample Sam's cheddar, Gouda, and something called a *burrata*, which turned out to be an outer layer of mozzarella with a soft center of mascarpone.

The food was as ambrosial as its culinary artist.

****

As raw weather settled into the narrow valleys of northern New York, Sam Richards wanted to hide from the bone-numbing chill and the mind-numbing season. He hated Christmas.

His scowl softened as he watched Maggie May, his border collie, herd the sheep into the barn for the night in a well-choreographed dance. The dog raced back and forth, oblivious to the bleating animals or the layer of snow on the ground, focused on her task. A sixth sense guided her to any sheep who drifted from the barn opening.

After the last straggling sheep entered the pen, Sam shut the barn door behind them and headed back to the house. Maggie May raced around him, wagging her tail, looking happy to be alive.

That makes one of us.

Snap out of it, Richards. His dad's voice echoed in his head. *You've got the family farm, the best piece of land in the whole county. Though why you had to get rid of the cows and get those mangy sheep, I'll never understand. Cows were good enough for your grandfather.*

Sam let the voice drift from his consciousness. He missed his dad, but encountered memories of him every day on land that had been in the family for generations.

The farm was part of Sam, too, entwined with his soul. When the guidance counselor in high school had asked his career plans, there was only one choice: run the family farm. The counselor had spent the next four years trying to talk Sam out of his decision.

Idiot.

The door to the farmhouse creaked in the cold. He stripped off his winter clothes in the mud room and thumped into the aging kitchen, successfully ignoring the fading linoleum, chipped porcelain sink, and cabinets needing paint.

Sweet aromas from the venison stew he'd started in the Crock-Pot that morning wafted around him, and he retrieved a bowl from the cupboard. His deer-hunting buddy, Charlie, had called the night before, letting him know he had more meat to barter for cheese.

The rhythms of country life, undisturbed by anything....or anyone. Sam had his books, his dog, and his livelihood, hard as it was. God painted a picture outside his door every morning.

He'd even been able to put most of the pain of the past behind him.

Other than getting better at making the best sheep's milk cheese in the country, his life could remain just the way it was.

The phone rang.

"Richards Handmade Cheese." He forced his voice to be calm and pleasant. *Calls at this hour might mean new orders.*

"Is this Sam Richards?" The woman's voice was sweet, but one he didn't recognize.

"Speaking."

"Oh, good! I was hoping it would be you. I have a proposition for you."

Probably not a new order. He'd had a few of these calls since that damn reporter interviewed him—women who thought he needed rescuing from a gloomy life, and who were prepared to do it.

He hadn't been *that* miserable looking during the television interview, had he?

Trying not to let his wariness carry into his voice, he asked, "How can I help you?"

"My name is Clara Misowski, and I have a tasting party business called The Perfect Plate, located in New Jersey. I make arrangements for groups of women to sample food directly from the source, like your cheese farm. The producer gives a demonstration of what he or she does, my clients sample your products, and buy something." Clara paused. "Well, most of the time they buy something. But never mind. You get publicity and I get paid to arrange the trip." She paused for a brief moment. "It's a win-win!"

He almost groaned aloud. A pack of women on his farm would be worse than being stuck in the barn with the sheep during a three-day winter storm. "Sorry, I'm..."

"No, don't hang up! Please...I mean..."

"Lady, I raise sheep. I make cheese. Occasionally, I force myself to market it." He gripped the phone tighter. "You saw the television interview, right?"

"Uh, yeah."

He tried to expel the gruffness from his tone. "You sound nice enough, but I'm not running an

153

entertainment center for a gaggle of women from...where did you say you were from?"

"New Jersey. Morristown."

Wherever that is. He made his voice polite, but firm. "I'm going to hang up now and feed my dog."

"What's the dog's name? She was so fun to watch on the TV."

He glanced at his dog who looked at him with alert brown eyes and thumped her tail.

"Maggie May. Now I..."

"I'd love to meet Maggie May. Can I at least come up and discuss this with you in person?"

"The answer will still be 'No.'"

"Please? I promise I won't take up too much time."

The scent of warm venison stew wafted toward him, and a pang of hunger hit his stomach. "Do whatever you want, lady. I gave you my answer."

❖Chapter Two❖

A few days later in the dim winter morning light, Clara drove north on Route 87 in her ten-year-old SUV. She was on a fool's errand, but she was determined to do whatever it took to get a cheese demonstration for her clients. At least, that's what she was telling herself.

The low rumble of his voice on the phone had been the kind of man-sound that made her insides all gooey; a growly bass that made her leap into situations without first examining possible consequences.

She needed to change her ways.

Right there, rumbling along the cracked cement highway, Clara made a vow. For the rest of her life, she would be the picture of a sober, practical, conservative businesswoman—as soon as she got Sam Richards out of her system.

She shoved Sam's image from her mind and forced it on her business. Six months into the venture, she was just breaking even. Women paid a fee to attend monthly outings. Clara made arrangements for the group to meet the people and experience the processes behind the food, beverages, and home products they enjoyed. Vendors paid her a percentage of everything they sold to her clients.

Visits to unique craft shops and art galleries inspired her clients to create their own fine dining experiences at home.

The trip to Roxbury would be her first long-distance culinary road trip with a group. Her mind whirled with the myriad of details required for the adventure. Should she rent a van for everyone for the long drive? Sharing a ride would keep them all together, although too much togetherness was a recipe for estrogen-fueled angst.

The wheels hummed over the pavement, and the snow along the sides of the highway increased. In Kingston, New York she turned onto Route 28, a two-lane highway that twisted and turned through the Catskill Mountains. A half hour later she pulled off the road at Woodstock, a town still living off the fame of a half-century-old music festival.

The arty town was still attractive. She noted a few places to research before satisfying her hunger with a turkey, Swiss cheese, and cranberry sandwich on thick brown bread. Then she headed deeper into the mountains and colder temperatures.

Patches of melting snow on the road forced her to slow down. *Maybe this trip should wait until summer.*

Dark evergreens iced with snow hung over the road. A buck at the edge of the road looked up, but didn't move, an idyllic reminder of Santa's reindeer. Her favorite season was only four weeks away.

Holidays get everyone in a spending mood. The group, and Clara's bank account, needed to make the trip in December. She'd make it work, snow or no snow.

A buzzing noise from her engine crashed into her anticipation of her first long-distance event.

Great. What's wrong now?

Clara's temples throbbed with the oncoming rush of a migraine. She gripped the steering wheel, and her knuckles whitened to the color of the snow around her. Was a wheel going to fall off, sending her plunging into a ravine? How long would it be before someone stumbled upon her lifeless body?

Or would a bear get her first?

A break in the trees gave her hope.

As she emerged from the pine-darkened mountains, she hunted the stark, white landscape for rescue. Plenty of scenic red barns and wide open spaces, but not a mechanic in sight. Nothing to do, but follow the directions Google Maps had provided for Richards Handmade Cheese and pray that she made it that far.

But what then? Would he be able to help her? Would he even want to help her? Or would they be snowed in until she could be rescued by a tow truck?

Her libido leapt at the thought of being trapped in an isolated farm with Sam Richards.

Sleet was falling by the time she reached the turn-off to the farm. The dirt road had been graded, so at least she didn't have to deal with ruts or potholes. As she drove down the lane toward the trim outbuildings, the buzz in her engine grew louder.

A barking dog—the one she'd seen on TV—bounded out to greet her.

A few seconds later, Sam came out of one of the buildings.

Her heart stopped. The real life version of her modern-day Heathcliff was much better than any fantasy.

Except the scowl across his face was larger.

Uh-oh.

He yelled something she couldn't make out. The motor clamor and the window glass muffled the words.

With a click, she turned off the engine and rolled down the window. "Hi!"

She tried to sound chipper, as if rolling into a stranger's driveway with a protesting vehicle was something she did every day.

He didn't answer, but the dog kept barking.

"Hush, Maggie May," he told the animal, his face softening a little. Then he returned his glare to Clara. "Who are you?"

"Clara Misowski." She smiled her perkiest smile.

"The same Clara who called the other day wanting to bring a herd of women to my farm?" He peered behind her to the rest of the SUV.

"That's me." She pushed her smile, hoping he liked dimples.

"Figures." His voice was gruff, but his expression relaxed a tiny bit.

Maybe the dimples worked.

****

The grinding noise of the maroon SUV as it had pulled down the driveway had curdled his day. He'd intended to send her on her way as soon as possible.

Then she rolled down the window and smiled.

Her heart-shaped face and high cheekbones were set off by a nose that wasn't quite perfect, and two smoky eyes. Her thick chestnut hair waved beneath a colorful knit cap, and her plump upturned lips gave a cautious smile that threatened to pierce the burnished armor cage he'd fastened around his emotions.

He forced himself to scowl more fiercely. "I told you I wasn't interested in entertaining."

"So you did." Her smile sweetened. She opened the car door and hopped out.

Damn.

Dressed in a mid-calf gray woolen skirt and pressed white shirt with a belted sweater, Clara looked like she could step from a fashion magazine, except Clara was all woman, not one of those skinny stick models.

Their eyes caught. The whisper of the wind rustling the barren limbs of the maples behind his house intensified the spell she wove around him.

His gaze dropped to her soft pink lips, and he fought the unexpected urge to kiss her.

No attachments, Richards, remember?

A *baa* came from the barn.

Her eyes widened, and she glanced around the yard.

He chuckled. "It's only a sheep."

"I know. Where are they?" Her voice sounded strained.

"In the barn." He cleared his throat. "Look, I'm sorry you wasted your time to come up here. Like I told you on the phone, I'm not interested in doing tours. I'm sure there are plenty of other cheesemakers out there who'd love to have your group visit." He glanced at his watch. "The Chamber of Commerce downtown should still be open. They'll be able to help you." He plastered a fake smile on his face, then was surprised to find he meant it. "Now, if you'll excuse me, I've got work to do." Forcing himself to turn his back on Clara, he headed toward the outbuildings.

"Wait!"

He did an about face.

She strode toward him. "There's something wrong with my car. Do you know a mechanic, or do I have to check the Chamber for that, too?" She glared at him.

Maybe if he fixed the problem, she'd be quicker to leave and he'd feel better about sending her on her way. "Ah, yes, the noise. Let me have a look." Machinery was a comfort, predictable to a point. No emotions were required to change spark plugs or replace a cracked piston.

She hovered as he lifted the hood of the SUV. "Better get back. Engines are messy work; a lot like raising sheep and making cheese. Not good for the fancy clothes you're wearing."

She backed off.

As he lifted the hood, he felt a chill in the air, and glanced toward the far ridge. A dark smudge of clouds told him snow was on its way.

He turned his attention to the engine, but couldn't see any obvious source of the grinding noise that had accompanied the car down the driveway. He needed to start the car to figure out the problem.

Swinging around to get the keys, he found himself a hand's breadth away from Clara.

"Do you know what you're doing?" she asked.

He laughed. "Most farmers and ranchers know mechanics. Comes with the territory."

She frowned. "You said you had things to do. I don't want to be a bother. I'll find my own mechanic. Town can't be that far away."

He was tempted to do as she asked, but glanced at the sky. The storm had crested the ridge. Who knew what kind of snow driving experience she had. Like as not, she'd drive into a ditch, or the car would stall, and he'd lose more of the day rescuing her than if he fixed the damn problem in the first place.

Besides, it would be a shame for her to ruin her clothes, although if her clothes were wet, she'd have to remove them to dry them off.

Richards, get a grip.

He took a deep breath. "The nearest mechanic is a long way off. Depending on what's wrong, you might not make it that far. Besides, there's a storm brewing." He pointed to the dark clouds steamrolling in their direction. "Why don't you start the car? I'll see if we can get this handled."

She stepped into the car.

❖Chapter Three❖

Clara perched on the driver's seat and started the engine.

The buzz started immediately so she turned it off.

"Leave it on!" Sam shouted.

She turned the car on again and cringed at the sound it made.

She took a look at the thickening clouds on the ridge and shuddered. Good thing Heathcliff had mechanical abilities.

"Off! Off! Didn't you hear me?" Sam banged on the car door. His scowl had returned, deeper than ever.

She silenced the engine. Blessed stillness.

Laughing, she slid off the driver's seat.

"What's so damn funny?" Sam asked.

Suddenly, she had enough of his moods. "This whole situation, that's what's funny. I came up here to spread some Christmas cheer, help you sell some of your cheese, and you act like Scrooge." She waved her arm at the bucolic setting. "You live in God's country and you're a grump."

A smile fought its way to the surface of his face. "Sorry. I'm always miserable this time of year. I can't wait for Christmas to be over."

"Why?" If Clara had her way, Christmas would last all year.

The frown returned. "Personal reasons."

"Oh."

The look on his face told her not to pry.

"Did you figure out what's wrong with the car?" she asked.

He nodded. "Transmission fluid's dirty."

"Dirty fluid is making that noise?" She'd have to get a real mechanic to look at the car.

"Yep. Unfortunately, the parts store is closed. You'll have to stay in Roxbury tonight."

Great. She got back into her car.

"Um, you probably shouldn't drive that until I change the fluid. You could ruin the transmission."

She blew out a puff of air. "What do you suggest I do then? It looks like a long walk to town."

He smiled, an actual real-live smile.

Miracles did occur.

"If you wait until I milk the sheep, I can run you into town." His grin broadened. "Want to watch? It's where the cheese actually begins."

Get into close confines with sheep? Not on her life. "I'll stay out here, if you don't mind."

He cocked his head. "They're sheep, one of the most harmless animals on earth—stupid as all get-out, but harmless. Why are you so afraid of them?"

Her cheeks warmed. "I fell into a pen on my uncle's farm once. They were really big and ran all around making those baaing noises."

"Big? Sheep?"

She grimaced. "I was four."

He laughed. It was a hearty laugh, and even though it was at her expense, it was a nice laugh. She caught a glimpse of the person he could be.

After he stopped laughing, he reached out his hand. "Let's get you over your fear of sheep."

She took a deep breath, once again a little kid facing her biggest fear.

The moment he touched her, the world tilted.

He must have been in the same universe, because he hesitated for a moment, as if he was shocked by his gesture. "Well," he said and looked into her eyes.

For a second, the shutters on his emotions dropped, and she saw the compassionate soul he truly was. His guard quickly fell back into place.

Tail wagging, Maggie May greeted them at the barn door. The dog sniffed Clara's hand, barked, and her tail swung more violently.

"I think she likes me," Clara said.

"Probably. She sees things most humans don't."

How was she supposed to take that? To be safe, she pulled her hand from his.

He frowned. "I didn't mean to offend you. Dogs are really smart. They get a good read on people—know who's good and who's bad."

"Oh." *Which does he think I am?*

He stared at her. "Guess you're one of the good ones." He held out his hand.

This conversation was getting too intense. She shook her head. "I'm fine."

He hesitated for a second, then led the way into the dim-lit barn.

Scents of hay, dust, and animal musk filled the air. As if sensing their arrival, the sheep started milling around and bleating.

Clara stopped in her tracks.

Sam turned to her. "You're not four anymore. The most they'll do is nuzzle you to death, or nudge you because they don't know enough to go around you." He out his hand again. "You're safe. Ready?"

She stared at him, reluctantly took his hand, and stepped toward the sheep.

****

Sam led her to the sheep pen, aware of the warmth of her hand in his. He shouldn't let her discomfort get to him, but he hated to see anyone afraid or hurt—even a woman who had disrupted his peaceful day.

"They're really round," Clara said with a tremor in her voice.

"Yeah. Especially this time of year. All that wool." He touched her hat. "Amazing that someone thought they could create something pretty out of all that dirty fiber."

He couldn't help himself. Her shiny hair drew his fingers like a full cookie jar had when he was a kid. He caressed a strand before he pulled his hand away.

"They're the ultimate herd animal." He led her closer to the pen. "When one does something, they all do the same thing. They are probably as scared of you as you are of them. Would you like to touch them? Feel their wool?"

Her face paled, but she straightened her shoulders. "Okay."

He guided her toward one of the ewes pressing against the pen slats. "This is Jenny, one of the older ewes. She won't mind if you touch her."

"How do you know which one's which?"

He pointed to a number painted on Jenny's back. "That makes them easy to identify. They also have ear tags, but they're hard to read from afar."

Clara slowly placed her hand on Jenny's back. The woman laughed; a tinkle of a sound. "It's stiff. I thought wool was soft."

Sam chuckled. "Once the wool is sheared off, it needs to be washed—a lot. There's a lot more than wool in what you're touching. Every piece of grass, straw or twigs they rub against manages to work its way into the top layers, and of course there's lanolin in there, too."

"Oh." Clara worked her hand up toward the sheep's head and brushed between the animal's ears.

Jenny turned her head and nuzzled Clara's hand.

"Soft!" Her laugh rang again. She turned and looked at him with bright eyes.

Her joy seared through a weak spot in his defenses. She seemed so like Hailey, so full of life and love. Before...

He pushed the thought away.

"Why don't you sit here while I get this job done and then I'll run you into town?" He led her to a hay bale.

166

He turned away from her while he went through the routine of cleaning the udders, attaching the milking machines, milking, and releasing the milking tubes from the ewes. About half-way through the hour-long chore, he heard a rustling. When he looked over, he saw she'd laid down on the hay and closed her eyes.

His barriers softened again. When she wasn't acting like a pushy businesswoman, she could be sweet. No matter how nice she was, though, he wouldn't do a demonstration for a colony of women.

After he finished his milking chores, he watched Clara sleep for a few minutes. What would it be like to have a woman like her to share his life? Over the past decade he'd constructed a precise way to get through his day. He'd convinced himself he was happy, but right now he wasn't sure.

Maybe he'd been fooling himself. Then remembered Hailey. He'd loved his kid sister and he'd lost her.

Her death was enough pain for a lifetime. Once he got Clara's car fixed, he'd send her out of his life.

❖Chapter Four❖

A touch startled Clara awake. "What?"

Where am I? She brushed bits of hay from her coat, hair, and hat as her memories returned.

She looked up. Sam Richards looked as delectable as in her dream, and, for once, he wasn't wearing a scowl.

She smiled. "I guess I fell asleep."

He nodded, his face softening even more.

A bleat startled her, and Clara focused on the pen. A black head protruded between two of the slats. "Poor thing. Looks like you're stuck." She walked to the enclosure, helped the animal twist its head, and released it from the fence.

"Guess you're not afraid of them anymore," Sam said.

She grinned. "Nope." She looked back at the sheep milling in the pen. "How come she couldn't get back out?"

"Told you. They're dumber than all get out." Sam took Clara's arm and steered her toward the barn door. "Let's get you into town and settled for the night."

After they put Maggie May inside the house, Sam led Clara to a driveway on the far side of the house. The pickup truck was clean on the inside, but the outside looked as though had taken a beating over the years.

Unlike her SUV, though, it started without sounding like a buzz saw.

He must have known what she was thinking.

"I always buy American-made. Lasts longer."

The truck rumbled down the drive.

"How did you get into making cheese?" she asked.

"When I went to college, I studied business along with Ag." He turned right onto the two-lane highway. "Those classes opened my eyes to reality. In order to make a living as a dairy farmer, especially on a small farm like the one I bought from my dad before he died, you have to be aware of the trends." He shrugged. "I knew I couldn't make money selling milk—all the big operations have taken over. Cheese was a different story. Artisan cheesemakers were doing well. Using sheep's milk instead of cow's milk gave my product an added distinction." He chuckled. "Of course, my dad was pissed. He'd owned cows all his life and couldn't understand why I wanted anything to do with 'dumb bleaters' as he called them."

"How are you doing?"

"It's a lot of work, but it gives me what I want."

"What's that?"

He gave her a sharp look. "To make a living and be left alone."

That's what she got for pushing her luck.

The thrum of studded snow tires took over the conversation for the next few miles.

"I'm sorry," she said in an attempt to regain his good graces. "I didn't mean to pry into your personal life.

You seem to have created a successful business—something that's escaped me up to now."

His hands were wrapped tightly on the steering wheel. "I have to admit your business sounds strange to me. I don't see how you could make a profit."

"Right now, it breaks even. It's like a tourist trip centered on food. The women pay me to make the arrangements, and I get a commission on the things that are sold. Remember, I told you that on the phone."

His lips flattened. "I wasn't paying much attention."

She stared at the Catskills. The threatening storm had crested the mountain ridge.

After a few seconds he said, "So let me get this straight. Not only would I have to put up with a group of women, which I already don't want, but I'd have to pay you for the privilege?"

Things weren't going well.

"Do you sell your cheese directly?" she asked.

"Rarely. The wheels are too big for most people, and I don't break them down."

She splayed her hands. "See? You wouldn't have to pay me anything because you wouldn't sell anything." Clara tried to add a light note to her voice.

"Well, that's a relief." His voice sounded sarcastic.

She glanced back at the storm which appeared to be steadily heading their way.

He chuckled. "I can see why you don't make any money."

She stared out the window at the moonlit snow-covered landscape, trying to recapture the enthusiasm she'd had moments before.

Maybe I am *a fool to think I can make The Perfect Plate work.*

She propped her elbow on the window ledge and rested her hand on it. *I should get a job, settle down, and be responsible.*

Her stomach churned. She'd had so much hope for her business.

Silence stretched on, but at least Sam's hands relaxed on the steering wheel.

Maybe it's not as bad as I think.

None of her previous business ventures had broken even before. There was still hope.

She stared out the window. The winds must have shifted because the storm appeared to be headed south, away from them.

When they rolled into the hamlet of Roxbury, her spirits lifted. Lights twinkled on railings and lampposts. Garlands and wreaths wrapped white clapboard houses, and Santa's sleigh dominated a large yard. Mullioned shop windows displayed Victorian Christmas scenes. Candlelit diners were framed by light-infused greenery at a classy-looking restaurant.

She wanted to stay in the town forever. "It's beautiful."

He grunted.

She turned to him. "Why are you so grumpy about Christmas?"

171

"I don't believe in it." He pulled into the driveway of a two-story clapboard house.

"Where are we going? I thought you were taking me to a hotel."

He shut off the engine. "We don't have any. There's a B & B way out of town, but it's usually booked this time of year. My friend Charlie and his wife Lucy started this inn a few months back. They should have a room for you."

"Oh. Okay." She opened the pickup door. "Are you Jewish?"

He laughed, got out of the truck, and walked around to the passenger side.

She started to get out.

"Watch your step. It's a long—"

She tripped on her skirt, knocked him into the bank of snow that lined the drive, and landed on top of him.

"I'm sorry. I didn't mean—" She looked into his eyes and found him staring at her, their faces only a few inches apart. Heat infused her, and she longed to touch her lips to his.

If this was a movie....

"Umm," he said.

...but it wasn't.

She pushed herself up and brushed off the snow before she did anything stupid. Besides, she'd promised herself no more risks. Level-headed women didn't kiss perfect strangers, especially men who hated Christmas.

If only he wasn't so sexy, and if only she wasn't a sucker for lost causes and dark brown eyes.

172

What would it take to get through to him, to make him believe again?

Sam stood up. "You okay?"

"I'm fine. How about you? You're the one I squished."

He wore an odd expression on his face; somewhere between hurt and joy. Then his features settled into a faint echo of the scowl she'd come to expect. "Maybe you should slow down a bit."

Then, unexpectedly, he smiled, as if he'd finally retrieved his manners. "Wouldn't want you to be hurt, you know."

Her steely resolve to be practical softened, and she smiled back.

He helped her onto pavement, and they walked toward the house.

Charlie and Lucy answered the door and ushered them into the foyer. Lucy, a small dark-haired woman, was dwarfed by her husband.

Sam explained the situation with Clara's car.

"You poor dear," Lucy said. "Of course we'll put you up. Why did you come to Roxbury?"

Clara gave her a brief overview of her venture, hoping Lucy would be more positive than Sam had been.

Lucy grabbed Clara's arm. "What a great business! We have to talk. I have so many ideas to make this town a destination spot. Your business could really help us out."

"She's on the town's board of directors." Charlie sounded apologetic. "Have you guys eaten dinner?"

Sam shook his head. "I'll get something together after I get home."

"But Clara has to eat," Lucy said. "We ate out tonight because we haven't had time to go grocery shopping yet. There's a new chef at the Roxbury Mill. It was fabulous! You should take Clara there tonight and make sure she eats, since you're the one who can't fix her car until tomorrow."

"But—"

Lucy turned to Clara. "You'll love the mill. It's full of shops. Great setting."

"Sounds wonderful," Clara said. "I'm starving." She glanced at Sam.

Scowling. No surprise there.

"Can I walk to the restaurant?" she asked.

Lucy frowned. "Not really."

Maybe if she paid for the meal...

"Would you mind coming to dinner?" she asked Sam. "My treat. It's the least I can do for the car repair."

"I don't think—"

"That's a wonderful idea." Lucy beamed. "Don't you think so, Charlie?"

Charlie looked like he'd rather be strung up by his toes than answer the question. "Well, it would solve the dinner problem." He grimaced a smile at Sam.

Sam glared at Charlie. "I guess I'm outnumbered. See you later, *friend.* Let's go, Clara. I'll get you fed and safely back to the inn."

She smiled. "Thanks."

"I'll bring her to your place in the morning," Charlie said. "Got to see the egg lady down your way."

****

174

Sam glanced at Clara's face as they pulled out of the driveway. Her expression reminded him of a small child the day before Christmas.

Like Hailey used to look.

The memory saddened him. All he wanted was to get home to Maggie May and forget, but Charlie and Lucy were right. Clara needed to have dinner, even if his friends had manipulated him into it. They always tried to set him up with some woman or another, and this one had fallen into their lap. Why couldn't they believe he didn't want to fall in love with anyone? Loving meant loss, the pain of someone wrenching his chest apart and pulling his heart out.

He was done with love.

As he turned down a side road by the river, he shut off the faucet of his memories and concentrated on the moonlit ripples of the water.

"Thank you." Clara's voice broke the silence, "for helping me out."

"It's what we do up here; help each other."

She touched his arm. "That may be true, but I know you'd rather be alone with your dog and your sheep."

He allowed himself to smile. "Well, maybe not the sheep..."

She chuckled.

Roxbury Mill appeared in the distance, nestled in a bend in the river. Several decades back, the old stone building had been converted from a non-working flour mill into small, exclusive enterprises. The restaurant changed hands periodically on its quest to fit into the ambience of the rest of the place.

Maybe the new chef would make a difference. Sam would have to contact him to see if he needed any cheese.

Lights twinkled on the iron railing lining the driveway and parking lot. Sam helped Clara out of the car—this time without mishap—and walked with her down the mostly-shoveled sidewalk as flakes drifted down from above.

"Wow!" Clara exclaimed. "This is so beautiful! I love it when winter's like this—the crunch of the snow underfoot, a few flakes sparkling in the night—I can even smell the snow, can't you?" She grabbed his arm and smiled up at him.

His determination to spend the rest of his life alone developed a hairline fracture.

I'd better get through this night quickly.

"If you lived here, winter wouldn't seem so romantic," he said, trying to dampen her enthusiasm.

"This is Christmas winter. That makes it magic!"

Joy radiated from her face and pierced his heart's armor like a laser, sending a smile to his lips. For a moment they simply stared at each other, as sparks bounced through his body.

Then he took her arm. "Shall we go in?"

The maitre d' sat them at a table near the stone fireplace with its gentle flames. Clara beamed with a happiness so contagious it began to seep into the hard-to-reach spots of his soul where the darkness lay.

She chattered about her plans for the holiday season, her company, and her family—at least five brothers and sisters, of which she was the youngest, by his count.

"What about your parents?" he asked.

Her lips turned down. "My dad was killed in a car accident a few years ago, right before Christmas. My mom hasn't really recovered. They'd been married thirty years. She's in a small apartment in a retirement community now. I see her two or three times a week."

"Don't your sisters and brothers help out?"

"They're scattered around the country with kids of their own. I'm the only one left in New Jersey." She smiled. "It's no problem."

He took a sip of wine before asking the next question. "How can you be so up about Christmas since your dad died around the holiday?"

Clara stared at him for a few seconds before she answered. "To do anything else would dishonor my father. He and my mom were—are—Christmas nuts. He'd dress up as Santa Claus every year. Keeping Christmas happy means keeping memories of my dad alive."

Sam sat back in his chair. Was he dishonoring Hailey by keeping Christmas like a reincarnation of Ebenezer Scrooge?

A waiter came over to take their orders.

After the waiter left, Clara asked, "What about you? How many siblings do you have?"

"Three." *This was territory best left behind.*

"Tell me about them. Are you the youngest?" She shook her head. "No, you wouldn't be. You're too serious. You have to be the oldest."

He nodded and cast about for another subject. "Where did you go to school?"

"Montclair State. I started out as an art teacher, but discovered I hated to teach—especially the school politics. Kids were okay, but most of them hated art."

"What did you do then?"

"I worked as a secretary in New York City for a while, and then I started a business." She frowned. "It didn't do so well."

The waiter brought soup to the table in a basic white tureen. "Soup is family-style," he said, "and comes complimentary with all dinners." He lifted the lid to reveal the deep aroma of onions and beef stock.

Clara drew in a breath. "Smells wonderful. I'll have to bring my group here for dinner." She smiled at Sam. "How can I convince you to show them your cheese making process? Maybe even give them a sample? Your cheese is available where a lot of them shop. It could increase your sales."

Her earnestness almost made him laugh. "Maybe I like the size of my company the way it is. Not everything needs to be bigger to be better."

Her eyes widened.

It seemed like a safe topic, so he continued. "If I got any bigger, I'd have to follow more regulations, get new equipment, and, worst of all, hire people." He shook his head. "Nope. I'm happy the way I am. You'll have to find another cheesemaker for your tour." He ladled soup

178

into her bowl and handed it to her before doing the same for himself.

Maybe eating dinner will keep her from asking too many questions.

She frowned and took a sip of her soup. "Wow. This is definitely the place to come." They ate in silence for a few moments. Then she put her spoon down, tilted her head, and smiled.

Uh-oh.

"If you don't want to do it for your business, could you do it for me? A cheese stop would round out the tour, especially if I combined it with the wine-tasting." If anything, her smile became broader. "That would be perfect. You could show them your process in your cheese cave—you have a cheese cave, don't you?"

He nodded.

"Then everyone could sample wine and cheese in there. It'd be fun."

"It'd be cold."

She touched his hand, tilted her head, and smiled. "Your participation would be a big help to me."

He had to laugh. "That work on your boyfriend?"

"I don't have a boyfriend." She grinned. "But it always got me what I wanted from my dad."

Her deep brown eyes brightened when she smiled, which increased her charm—and danger.

"So what happened to your first business?" he asked.

She placed a spoonful of soup into her mouth, closed her eyes, and hummed her approval. After she'd swallowed, she said, "It failed. Like the second one. As you so helpfully pointed out earlier, I don't handle the money aspect of business well. That's why I need your help. I don't know what I'll do if this business fails, too. I'll have to go back to slaving in an office. Please help me."

The winsome look was back.

He felt like a heel, but shook his head anyway. "I can't. Let's just leave it at that."

❖ Chapter Five ❖

Admitting defeat wasn't in Clara's nature, but she'd done everything she could to make the man agree, and hard as it was, it was time to give up.

But the spirit of the season *must* linger in his soul somewhere. If only she could get that spark to light, magic would take care of the rest—she felt *sure* of it.

As they finished their meal, the conversation meandered through the mundane.

"I'd better get you back to the inn before they lock you out," he joked after the waiter returned with her credit card and receipt.

"They won't really do that, will they?"

He chuckled and shook his head. "No, I'm kidding."

"I knew there was a sense of humor in there somewhere." She looked at him from under her eyelashes. *Damn, he's good-looking.*

She could almost hear her mother's sensible voice.

What are you thinking, girl? You can barely keep your business going. You've got no time for romance—especially with a prickly pear who lives three hours away.

It was time to heed her mother's pragmatic approach to life. Once the car was fixed, Clara would leave Roxbury and never look back.

They left the restaurant and walked past the shops toward the outer door. She spotted a store in a corner she hadn't noticed on their way in. Christmas beamed from its windows. Best of all, it was open.

"Oh, look!" she exclaimed. "I have to go in."

He scowled. "I don't. I'll wait for you on this bench."

She put her hands on her hips. "Really?"

He sat and leaned against the wall behind the polished wooden bench. "Really."

"Okay, your loss."

"Uh-huh."

She left him and walked into the store.

Not surprisingly, the proprietor looked like Mrs. Santa Claus with a warm personality to match. "Take all the time you want, dearie. We have some lovely things from our local craftspeople."

Clara examined artistically created ornaments reflecting the countryside around them, quilted wall hangings, and woven throws. Knitted scarves entwined with holiday colors and matching hats enthralled her. Hand-carved rustic miniature villages lined the walls, complete with people, animals, and a dog who looked just like Maggie May, pulling a sled with four small children.

Without thinking of the possible consequences, she purchased the dog and sled, along with one of the scarves. She'd give the carving to Sam tomorrow after her car was fixed. He may not be willing to host her group, but he'd remember her.

"What'd you get?" he asked, standing when she returned to the bench.

She pulled out the scarf and showed him.

He examined the tag and nodded. "I thought that was Ursula's work. She lives north of here. She buys a few fleeces from me, then spins, and dyes them by hand. It's gorgeous craftsmanship."

"It is."

"What else is in the bag?"

"Nothing important. I think we should go now."

He eyed her for a few moments. "Okay."

Neither of them spoke on the short ride back to the inn.

"You don't have to help me out," she said and pulled up the door handle.

"Right." He hopped out of the truck's cab and came around. "I've seen you try to get out of this thing. Besides, around here, a man walks a woman to the door at night." He grinned. "I wouldn't want a rogue deer to get you or something like that."

"Do you have many rogue deer here?" She strolled next to him, and hoped to prolong the few steps to the door.

"Depends on whether or not they get a whiff of a city girl."

"Well, I'm not really a city girl, so I should be safe."

They stopped by the door, and he gently spun her toward him. "I could have sworn you are a bona fied, gussied-up, never-seen-a-sheep-in-her-life city girl." His voice was low and husky.

"Remember, I was intimately acquainted with sheep at an early age." She tilted her head up to see him better.

The air charged with longing.

"I seem to recall that." His face was close to hers, his expression sober.

She looked into his eyes and caught a glimpse of hope. Her heart swelled with anticipation.

He bent down and brushed her lips with hers. His lips tasted of fresh air with a hint of the coffee he'd had after dinner. This close, she caught a whiff of his aftershave, an outdoors piney smell.

She hungrily responded, but he stiffened and broke off the kiss.

"I'm sorry. That was a mistake." He took a step back. "I'll see you tomorrow when Charlie brings you for your car."

She licked her lips, savoring his taste, and stifling her shame.

"Goodnight then." He walked back to his truck.

She opened the door and gave one more glance in his direction.

He was standing by the truck as if he was waiting until she went inside.

Damn him.

With dignity, she walked into the inn and shut the door behind her. It took every ounce of strength she had to keep from crying until she got to her room.

The next morning, Clara took a brief shower and changed into the clean clothes she'd brought from New Jersey "just in case." Although she'd planned to make the trip to Roxbury from Morristown in one day, she liked to be prepared for anything.

Make-up hid the circles under her eyes from a restless sleep.

Breakfast was a custom-made omelet, sautéed vegetables, and a golden muffin served in a re-created colonial dining room replete with maple furniture and knick-knacks.

Lucy sat down with her while she ate. "Can you tell me about The Perfect Plate? The concept intrigues me. I took some business classes in college and I may have some ideas for you."

"That would be great! I can use all the help I can get." Clara smiled. "I like to entertain and create the perfect setting for a meal. Inviting people who will mesh together is important, too. Friends wanted me to cater events for them. I tried that for a while." She shrugged. "But being responsible for all the minutia of what went on every second was too stressful. I lost the reason I loved to do it in the first place."

The omelet cut easily with her fork. She scooped a cheesy slice of heaven into her mouth. "Oh, yum." She took another bite before answering Lucy's question. "I like to discover things—like your amazing inn— and share them with others. I was surfing the web one day and I saw someone in California had created a business out of doing exactly that. She called it The Joyful Table. It sounded perfect."

Another forkful of omelet entered Clara's mouth, and its exquisite taste stoked her enthusiasm for her business. "I started six months ago. Members pay a fee, and artisans pay me a commission on what they sell to my group. I began to think about all the amazing craftspeople there are in New York and New England, as well as south toward Virginia, and I realized I could expand it to weekend trips with stays in unique inns, like this one."

Lucy clapped her hands. "What a fabulous idea! I'd love to have your group stay here."

Clara grinned. After all the nay-sayers, it was nice to find someone who didn't think she and her idea were crazy.

"Like Charlie told you, I'm on our town's board of directors," Lucy said. "Roxbury is a great tourist destination. We have the scenery, and there are plenty of artists around here. Actually, any place in the Catskills or Finger Lakes region would be ideal, but not as good as Roxbury." She grinned and sipped her coffee. "Have you ever thought about expanding to website sales?"

"Not really. I'm not sure how that works."

"Me either, but I'll think about it and send my ideas along by email. You can tell me what you think. And we can figure out the best arrangements for your guests, too."

Clare smiled. "That would be great." She turned the expression to a frown. "There's only one problem. Sam adamantly refuses to talk to the group about cheese making."

Lucy laughed. "Sam's not the only craftsman in town." She got up and ruffled through a basket of

186

business cards. "Here." She handed several cards to Clara. "Heidi makes honey, Drake crafts baskets, and Hassan does ceramics. I'm sure they'll all be open to your idea."

Clara smiled, but sadness sat in her stomach. If she didn't get to spend time with Sam, how would she be able to reignite his spirit?

She ate a few slices of the Clementine artfully arranged on her plate, savoring the sweet juices. "What is it with Sam? Why is he so grumpy? And why doesn't he like Christmas?"

Lucy tapped her mug. "He claims he doesn't want any attachments. Charlie grew up here with Sam and says Sam used to be different, before..." She pursed her lips closed.

"Before what?"

Shaking her head, Lucy said, "It's not my story to tell. You'll have to ask Sam. Let's just say something awful happened one Christmas and he's never recovered."

"How long ago?" Clara asked.

"I think it was his freshman year in college."

"Some time ago?"

"Yes." Lucy looked up from her study of her coffee and locked eyes with Clara. Slowly, a smile blossomed across her face. "Too long. It's time for him to rediscover what the holidays are all about."

Clara smiled in return. "I couldn't agree more."

I'm not done with you yet, Sam Richards.

****

Sam had changed the transmission fluid before Charlie delivered Clara to his house, hoping to speed her on her way, but as soon as she stepped out of Charlie's Jeep, his heart gave an unfamiliar lurch.

The jeans and plum sweater she wore revealed more of her body than the fashionable skirt she'd worn the day before. Her figure was trim and curvy in all the right places, but it was her smile that tugged at his emotions. Her expression promised the world.

Maybe it was time to stop running from life. If she could get over her father's Christmas accident, then...

He shoved the thought from his mind. His situation was totally different.

Totally.

Charlie called out the Jeep window. "I've gotta go. Once I return with the eggs, Lucy has a honey-do list as long as my arm."

Sam grinned and waved.

Clara walked to him with a backpack, purse, and paper bag in her hands.

"You're ready to go," he said pointing to the SUV. He made his voice as gruff as possible to hide his churning emotions.

"That's wonderful. Thank you."

He stepped back, afraid she might throw her arms around him with gratitude. The kiss last night had been a huge mistake. He'd spent most of last night trying to figure out what had come over him, to ensure it didn't happen again.

"How much do I owe you for the fluid?" She placed the paper bag on the hood of her car and fumbled through her purse.

"Put that away. You treated me to dinner last night. That's enough."

She looked up at him, her eyelashes thick around her deep brown eyes.

He opened the driver's side door to her SUV. "You should be fine to get back to New Jersey now."

Leave. Please. Leave so I can pretend to be happy again.

"I have this for you." She handed him the paper bag. "I got it at the shop last night."

He clenched his jaw. "I don't believe in Christmas, remember? Give it to someone who'll appreciate it."

She really needed to leave.

"I think you're fooling yourself, Sam Richards. Why don't you open it and see? It reminded me of you."

Reluctantly, he opened the bag and drew out the paper-wrapped object.

"Open it." The grin lit up her beautiful eyes.

Slowly, he unwrapped the paper bag and exposed a border collie pulling four children on a sled.

"There are four of you, like you told me," Clara said. "You and your brothers and sisters!"

Bile rose in his throat and his hand griped the carving a little too hard.

The dog's tail broke off and fell to the ground.

"One died," he managed to choke out. "There's only three now." He stuffed the gift back in the bag, picked up the dog's tail, and threw it in. "Hailey died at

Christmas. My beautiful teenage sister died because I talked my parents into letting her go skiing." He glared at Clara. "Now, do you get it? I don't want pain like that again—not from you or anyone else. Can't you go away? Just go!"

Turning away to hide the tears that threatened to fall, he stalked back to his house, unaware he still had the paper bag in his hand.

The engine of Clara's SUV started up smoothly.

At least I can do something right.

❖ Chapter Six ❖

Over the next week, Sam did the bare minimum to keep his animals cared for and his business running. He avoided town and drove to Stamford, thirteen miles each way, to get his supplies.

One evening, about a week after Clara left, he heard a knock on the back door. A moment later, the door opened, and Charlie walked in with a six-pack of beer.

And a wreath.

"You can take that back with you." Sam pointed at the greenery.

"Stop being such a jerk," Charlie replied as he took out two bottles and placed them on the table. The rest of the beer went in the refrigerator.

"It's my house. I can be whatever I want." Sam hung the towel over the oven door handle.

"Lucy says 'no.'"

Sam laughed. "I don't have to answer to Lucy. You do."

Charlie slid him a beer. "She's coming back, you know."

"Who?" Sam knew damn well who Charlie meant.

"Clara. She and Lucy put their heads together and came up with a scheme for The Plate whatever—"

"Perfect Plate."

"Yeah."

"I told Clara I wouldn't do it." Sam pulled out his kitchen table chair. The beer was his favorite—Sam Adams.

"They're working around you being a jackass."

Sam slugged back a mouthful of beer. *Why can't people leave me alone?* "They can do whatever they want as long as they don't include me or—" he gestured at the wreath— "or try to force Christmas on me."

Charlie folded his hands on the table and stared at Sam. "Hailey died ten years ago, Sam. She'd hate to see you like this."

Sam pushed his chair back, stood, and walked to the sink. He leaned against it and drummed his fingers on the porcelain. "She wouldn't have died if not for me."

Charlie shook his head in exasperation. "I can't believe how many times we've been over this, and you still won't let it go. Sometimes I think we should get one of those—what do you call them?—dominatrices to beat it out of you."

The image was so startling and unexpected, Sam laughed. Charlie joined in. The laughter boiled up from every part of Sam's being, sparked by the tiny flame Clara had lit the week before. Soon Sam was on the floor, arms around his knees, roaring.

Suddenly, everything changed. The hiccups of hysteria gave way to the sobs of pain.

Charlie climbed down on the floor next to him.

"If only I hadn't told Mom and Dad to let her go." Sam's words staccatoed between sobs.

"She would have wheedled her way on that ski trip. You know that. She was eighteen and had your dad

192

wrapped around her little finger. After three sons, your dad didn't stand a chance."

"But—"

"It was an accident, Sam. Two kids collided. It wasn't your fault. Why can't you believe that? Why can't you stop punishing yourself?"

Sam forced himself to consider the question as he got his sobs under control. He rested his back against the cabinet and re-imagined the scene from that long ago night.

He'd gotten home for his first Christmas break the evening before. Immediately, Hailey had started badgering him for support to go on the holiday ski trip with the senior class.

"Mom's got one of her bad feelings," she'd whined. "She doesn't want me to go. Dad's wavering, I can tell. All they need is a little push from you, big brother, and I'm golden."

He'd laughed and acceded to her wish.

She'd gotten her ski trip, and the unthinkable had happened. Racing down a slope, she'd run into a high school linebacker. Her neck had snapped.

Sam didn't have a chance to say good-bye.

It was the last Christmas he'd ever celebrated.

Charlie stood, gave Sam a hand up, and passed him a beer.

"Thanks, bro," Sam said, "not just for the brew, but the question." He leaned back in the chair and studied the table. "Living the way I have seemed like something I needed to do. Maybe I thought if I did it long enough, she'd come back."

He wiped his eyes. No use bawling like a baby again.

"It doesn't work that way," Charlie said.

Sam shook his head. "I know that, but I haven't been willing to give up my hair shirt."

"What's different now?"

A set of dark eyes framed by feathered eyelashes appeared in his mind. Could it be that simple? Was the desire to live again started by nothing more than an attractive woman?

"Lucy likes her." Charlie grabbed another beer from the fridge.

Sam smiled. "Clara *is* enthusiastic—and very reluctant to accept 'no' for an answer."

"Maybe you shouldn't give it to her then."

Sam leaned forward. "She told me the damndest thing."

"What?" Charlie took another slug of his beer.

"Her dad died before Christmas."

"It doesn't seem to have stopped *her* enthusiasm for the holiday."

Sam shook his head. "Nope. It hasn't."

Charlie stood up and placed his bottle in the recycle bin before he shrugged into his jacket.

"Don't forget your wreath," Sam said, as he got up from his chair.

"Lucy will skin me alive if I come back with that thing." Charlie looked steadily at Sam. "Christmas is the season of light and hope, Sam. Why don't you try letting a little of it into your own life for a change?"

194

Sam glanced at the wreath Charlie had laid next to a crumpled paper bag on the old work table at the far end of the kitchen.

"Maybe I will."

****

Shortly before Christmas, Clara drove back to Roxbury. The woods and fields lining the road were heavier with snow than they'd been a few weeks before. Red barns and gray silos in the distance added to the season's picturesque beauty.

The tires thrummed on the cleared pavement, and she sang along to the Christmas tunes coming from her sound system. The engine was blessedly quiet. This trip would be a financial and joyful success. She could feel it in her bones.

With Lucy's help, she'd pulled together a website to promote the artisans she'd worked with around New Jersey. Most had been enthusiastic, and orders were already rolling in. Between that income and the culinary road trips, success seemed to be within her grasp.

She'd taken a gamble by planning the trip to upstate New York in the winter, but ten women had signed up within the first twenty-four hours, and five more were on a waiting list for the next trip she planned.

Brainstorming with Lucy had given her ways to tweak the trip and its aftermath to make the concept even more financially rewarding. After talking frequently by phone with her newfound friend over the past few weeks, Clara realized she really needed a partner.

A thrill of anticipation ran through Clara. Depending on how the weekend went, she'd approach Lucy on Sunday about becoming a partner in The Perfect Plate.

Only one dim light remained. Clara hadn't heard from Sam. After she'd returned home from her visit to Roxbury, she'd emailed him an apology for overstepping her boundaries.

She'd received nothing but silence in return.

The inn was decorated for Christmas: light-entwined greenery looped on the picket fence, a huge wreath on the door and single electric candles in the mullioned windows. Her clients would be delighted.

Lucy greeted her with a warm hug. "It's so good to see you again. Why don't you settle in your room and then you can come downstairs? I have tea, cookies, and a surprise for you."

"A surprise? Can't you tell me now?"

An impish grin played across Lucy's face. "Nope. Scoot."

Clara's heart beat with excitement. She loved surprises, no matter how large or small.

She hung up her few things and trotted back down the stairs to the dining room. "What is it?"

Lucy laughed. "You're a little kid, aren't you?"

Clara smiled and splayed her hands. "It's more fun to view the world like a big present I get to unwrap every day. I hate to see people promote doom, gloom, and strife—especially at Christmas. I mean, *really*. It's the season of hope and anticipation. No matter what happened, my parents always believed life could get better." She sat down. "So what's my surprise?"

"It should be here any moment." Lucy poured tea. "In the meantime, let's review what each of your guests will need—breakfasts, snacks, that kind of thing. This is such a great idea, Clara. I'd like to do it again in the spring for the flowers, and late summer when the vegetables come in. What do you think?"

For the next hour, Clara and Lucy solidified plans for the clients due to arrive the following Friday afternoon. All the while the imminent arrival of a surprise teased Clara's brain.

The front door opened around five, followed by the clump of boots coming down the hall.

When Sam poked his head into the dining room, Clara's heart took a little leap.

Still as good-looking as he was two weeks ago.

Then she gave him a closer look. Something had changed. His face looked more relaxed.

He grinned. "Are you just going to stare at me like I'm one of Santa's elves, or are you going to say hello?"

"Hello!" She leapt from her chair and walked to him. "Are you my surprise?" She wanted to hug him, but hesitated when she remembered their last encounter. "*You* made a Christmas joke?"

He laughed. "Amazing, isn't it? Let's sit down. I want to see if you can fit my cheese making operation into the busy schedule Lucy says you have."

Stunned, Clara sat. "You've changed your mind?"

"Yes, about a lot of things." His gaze lingered on her face, giving shades of meaning to his statement.

Lucy cleared her throat. "I think, if you get started a half hour earlier and plan dinner a half hour later, you can squeeze Sam in right before the candlemaker on Saturday. I know the candle shop is pretty flexible with its schedule, and I've already checked with the restaurant, and they're okay with the adjustment. What do you think?"

"I think that sounds perfect," Clara said. She looked at Sam. *What happened to him?*

They finalized arrangements for the event.

"Can you come with me?" Sam asked when they were finished. "I have something I want to show you at my place. Besides I'm sure you'd love to see the sheep again." He chuckled.

"Sheep?" Lucy asked Clara.

"I was afraid of them, but once Sam showed me how docile—"

"And dumb," Sam added.

"—and *cute* they are, I got over it. Now I see them as future woolen hats."

Lucy smiled. "Have fun, you two."

❖Chapter Seven❖

Clara kept the conversation light on the way to Sam's house. The last thing she needed was for him to blow up again like he did when she'd given him the carved dog and sled. While he seemed different to her, she didn't trust miraculous transformations, even if it was Christmas. Instead, she focused on how she'd prepared for the weekend, creating a pamphlet for attendees that included maps and history behind each activity.

"Of course, you've gone and ruined it. I have nothing about you to give them." she jokingly complained.

"Sometimes you can plan too much," he said.

She laughed. "That may be true, but when you have ten women to shepherd around town, planning counts. Even then, you're bound to lose one because she has to use the bathroom or something."

"Sheep are easier."

"You have your dog."

He smiled. "You could borrow her."

"I think the women would object to Maggie May nipping at their heels."

"Probably." He turned down the long drive to his farm.

As they drew closer she was startled to see the side of his red barn lit by a floodlight. An enormous green circle was suspended in the circle of light. "A wreath?"

"There's another one on the front door."

"What happened? I knew something was different, but you were so opposed to Christmas."

"Let's go inside and I'll explain."

When he helped her out of the truck, the warmth from his hand traveled up her arm and added to the heat inside her. Once she landed on the ground, she stood still, and took in the moment: starlit skies, full moon, white snow, red barn, green wreath, and Maggie May running to greet them.

The crimson of his lips as he lowered them to hers.

She melted into his kiss. It lasted long enough to give her a taste of the man, but was too short to satisfy her.

"That," he said, "was not a mistake."

She smiled, finally believing in the miracle.

The magic of Christmas really could heal a broken heart.

They joined hands and walked to the house, Maggie May trailing behind them, tail wagging.

Once they got inside, he helped her off with her coat. "Tea? Coffee? Glass of Chardonnay?"

"The wine would be nice. I drank gallons of tea with Lucy." She glanced around at the tidy, but old-fashioned kitchen. "So this was your parents' house?"

"Yeah. Someday I'll remodel, but right now the business is taking up all my time."

"I get that." Suddenly, she saw the dog and sled she'd given him a few weeks before, centered in the middle of fake snow on his sideboard. "You fixed the tail!" She clapped her hands with delight.

"Yes. A little glue will do wonders, and Maggie May needs a tail to wag."

The dog in question barked.

Sam handed her the wine and offered, "Have a seat."

They sat at the kitchen table, and each took a sip of wine, their gazes never leaving each other.

"Mmm. It's good," she said, wondering what he wanted to tell her.

"It's from the winery you're visiting tomorrow." He rubbed his fingers over the condensation on the glass. "I'm sorry I got so upset with you last time. I haven't celebrated Christmas since my freshman year in college."

She touched his arm, hoping to ease some of the pain evident in his eyes. "What happened?"

He twisted his glass in his hands. "Hailey was a high school senior. A bunch of her friends were going for a skiing weekend in Vermont the weekend between Christmas and the New Year, and she wanted to go. My parents waffled."

He sipped his wine.

She stayed silent.

"I convinced them to let her go." His dark brown eyes clouded with pain. "It was the worst mistake of my life. She...she..." His eyes watered. "There was an accident. They...they said she died immediately."

"I'm so sorry." Clara rubbed his arm.

They sat quietly for a few minutes.

"Why now? How come you're finally able to let the pain go?" she asked.

He smiled. "First you came along with your belief in Christmas cheer no matter what happens." He placed his hand on hers. "When you told me about your dad I couldn't believe you still celebrated Christmas. It didn't make any sense to me.

"Then Charlie asked me a question I didn't really have an answer to. Why was I still punishing myself? Hailey wouldn't have wanted me to. So I spent the better part of a week thinking about that question."

"And?"

A brief smile crossed his face. "I think I'm dumber than the sheep." He sobered. "Somewhere in my adolescent brain I decided if I punished myself long enough, I'd make up for Hailey's death. In some stupid way I guess I even thought my sacrifice would bring her back to life. I finally saw the only way to make her life worthwhile was to start living my own."

She let the silence linger, but kept her hand on his arm.

"I realized during the weeks you were away, if I didn't change that belief, I'd just be a shell, communing with a dog and some sheep for the rest of my life."

He put his hand over hers and rubbed his thumb on it. "You walked into my life a few weeks ago and turned it upside down. You had so much joy in the simple act of breathing. The contrast with my own black and white version of life came into focus. After you left, it was like the sun went out."

Without letting go of her hand, he stood and pulled her up next to him. "I'd like to celebrate Christmas this year. With you. Is that possible?"

She smiled. "You're an answer to prayer. My mother informed me she was tired of watching me bounce from one thing to another without ever producing grandchildren. She's off to visit my brother in Denver for the holiday."

She took a risk and put her arms around his waist. "I have one more condition."

"What's that?" He gave her a mock scowl.

She feathered a kiss across his lips. "I want to tie red ribbons around the sheep."

The dog barked.

"Maggie May wants one, too."

"Of course."

"It's a deal." He lowered his head to hers and kissed her.

Epilogue

The following spring…

"It's so good to see you, Lucy!" Clara dumped her suitcase on the dining room floor and threw her arms around her friend and business partner. "I'm sorry it's been so long."

"Not a problem." Lucy returned the hug. "You've been busy."

"I know. I've hired someone in New Jersey to handle the tasting tours there while I concentrate on culinary road trips. That idea you had about starting a website to showcase the partners of The Perfect Plate was absolutely brilliant! With the money we're getting from ads and commissions from the sales, we've reached a whole new level of revenue. We're going to be a success!"

Clara twirled around in joy. Not only was she doing what she loved, she was actually making money.

"It's all your doing." She pointed at Lucy.

Lucy shook her head. "We each bring something. That's what collaboration is all about." She smiled. "Enough about that. When are your guests supposed to arrive for the tour?"

"Tomorrow around noon. Rooms ready?"

Lucy nodded.

Clara looked at the floor. "Um—do you mind if I stay a few extra days? I need to look for an apartment." She looked up and caught Lucy's grin.

"About time. Sam's intolerable after he comes back from seeing you in New Jersey. What about your mother, though? Will she be willing to move up here?"

Clara shook her head. "She's not coming. After she spent Christmas with my brother and his family in Denver, she decided Colorado was the place to be. She's the happiest I've seen her since my dad died. Next thing I know she'll find a beau."

Lucy laughed. "Good for her. Since she's not moving here, I have an idea. There's a small studio apartment at the back of the inn. We'd planned to upgrade it when the inn made a profit and rent it to long-term guests."

"I'd be in your way."

"Nonsense! Besides—" Lucy gestured toward the hallway behind Clara. "I don't think you'll be here for long."

Clara turned around to see Sam in the doorway, a fistful of daisies in his hand, and a big grin on his face. Maggie May sat by his side.

"Good to see you smiling, Sam." Lucy walked toward the kitchen. "I'll leave you two alone."

Sam held out his arms, and Clara went into his embrace.

He closed his arms around her.

She looked up at his face, his cragginess softened by his own spring of rebirth. He no longer resembled the love-mad Heathcliff.

"I love you," she said.

"I love you too, Clara."

As they kissed, Maggie May ran circles around them, barking her approval.

No, Clara wouldn't be staying at the inn for long.

ABOUT THE AUTHORS

Danica Winters

Danica Winters is a bestselling author who is known for writing award-winning books that grip readers with their ability to drive emotion through suspense and often a touch of magic. When she's not working, she can be found in the wilds of Montana testing her patience while she tries to understand the allure of various crafts (quilting, pottery, and painting are not her thing). She always believes the cup is neither half full nor half empty, but it better be filled with wine.

Jennifer Conner

Jennifer Conner is a bestselling Northwest author who has over thirty short stories on ebook and three full-length books in print. She writes in Contemporary Romance, Paranormal Romance, Historical Romance, and Erotica. Shot in the Dark hit Amazon at #1 in Romantic Suspense and Christmas Chaos was #2 in the Romance category. Her novel Shot in the Dark was a finalist in the Emerald City Opener, Cleveland, and Toronto RWA contests. Jennifer is an Associate Publisher for the indie e-book company Books to Go Now that resides in the Seattle area.

Sharon Kleve

Sharon Kleve was born and raised in Washington and currently lives on the Olympic Peninsula with her husband. Sharon Kleve loves romance. She loves reading romance, living romance, and especially loves writing about romance. She gets no greater feeling than watching her characters come alive in each other's arms. Most of all, she loves giving her characters the happily ever after they deserve--with a few bumps and bruises along the way. One of her favorite things to do is picking up a new book and sinking into the story, immersing herself in the emotions between the characters. She hopes to inspire her readers the same way her favorite authors have inspired her. When not writing, she can usually be found either curled up in her recliner with her cat and a good book, or in the kitchen baking sourdough bread or bagels.

Casey Dawes

Casey Dawes writes and quilts on the Clark Fork River in Missoula, Montana where she spends far too much time watching wildlife from her "woman cave." She shares her peaceful abode with a husband she adores and two cats who think they own the joint. In her previous "lives" she's been a medical records secretary, stagehand, college professor, junior high teacher on an Indian Reservation, Montessori teacher in Brooklyn, temp in businesses in New York City, a database guru for several fortune 500 companies, business and life coach. She's lived in New Jersey, Massachusetts, Michigan, Montana, New York City, Pennsylvania and California. With these varied careers, four step-children and two boys of her own, she has plenty to write about! She's written three non-fiction books

6781712R00125

Made in the USA
San Bernardino, CA
18 December 2013